THE TIME FUSE AND THE POWDER KEG

James Schombs

Published in the United States of America

ISBN 978-1-962569-34-7 (SC)
ISBN 979-8-89395-992-5 (Ebook)

Schombs and Schombs Publishing
222 West 6th Street
Suite 400, San Pedro, CA, 90731
jschombs.2k@gmail.com

Ordering Information and Rights Permission:

Quantity sales. Special discounts might be available on quantity purchases by corporations, associations, and others. For details, contact the publisher at the address above.

For Book Rights Adaptation and other Rights Permission. Call us at toll-free 1-888-945-8513 or send us an email at admin@stellarliterary.com.

Contents

Summary

Intellectual thinking and the use of imagination bring new ideas to fruition. There are many devices that can be modified to meet the user's desired outcome. Remote control toys and vehicles are an example. Military and tactical equipment are all brought to us by these new ideas! Research, Development, Testing, and Evaluation (RDT&E) have brought us many new technologies. Scientific exploration has put us on the moon!

Some of the ideas that are used in this story may be available for special-purpose uses. Why not counter an enemy technology or system with a system that prevents the enemy device from functioning as designed?

Thomas Edison with his invention of the light bulb and Henry Ford with the automobile have made the public's lives easier and more modern. This modern age is working in most of the world.

But some areas do not believe in modernization due to religious beliefs or a sense of denial.

Situational awareness and creative thinking can turn new ideas into creative inventions. Tactics have evolved over time from experiencing them in action.

This story is about a group of Special Operations warriors who have retired. There comes a day when one must ask, "How much is too much?" And when the answer is "We've reached that point," a person must stop it and put an effective end to the problem. This story is considered to be a fact/fiction novel and the reader can determine what they feel is or could be fact or is simply fiction from the imagination of the author?

When leadership is strong and effectively accomplishing the best for the nation and the public, then everything is good. When a leader is weak and ambiguous, then the nation becomes uncomfortable and suffers with a weak economy and a weak appearance that the whole world can see from the nation's internal problems. Over-taxation and an out-of-control public debt are signs of poor leadership.

That is when some must stand up again to correct the direction on the compass so that our ship does not wreck against rocky shores. These patriots reconnect in an effort to make this global war end in their victory and thus the defeat of terrorism! This book tells how their plan was carried out. This is an introduction to this special team, who gave up their retired lives to return to the life of stealth and special operations! Some things just need to be made right sometimes! They call themselves Team Jaguar. This is their story. Predator is part of team Jaguar and narrator for this story

For the most part, these guys did not feel comfortable being back in the civilian world again. They always felt like they were late for a meeting; they felt a sense of urgency to do something. They constantly needed to go for a run or swim, lift weights, anything to keep their minds occupied and their muscles and adrenalin pumping.

They also all felt some loss in their hearts. The Special Operations Forces community is a very tight-knit, special group of men and women. The camaraderie is similar to family. When someone loses a person who was close to them or loved by them, they can understand somewhat how this feels.

These men selflessly committed themselves in honor of the warriors who did not make it back—or who did come back, but are paralyzed or in wheelchairs! There are many who have lost a limb and been retrofitted with the finest prosthetics available today. These warriors understand why the Team Jaguar guys volunteered to complete the mission that had been terminated by politicians who never provided enough time for our forces to win!

Having a void of emptiness in your heart is a horrible feeling. Some veterans are placed on medications, while others see therapists. Mental health becomes an issue for some from traumatic experiences in combat or visions of death.

The warrior life really never fully leaves you for good. Every once in a while, you may awake from a dream drenched in sweat! That is just how it is. Depression attempts to attack the majority. Most beat it away while some cannot block the thoughts and are placed on medications or hospitalized to help the with this problem.

This story begins in the far past and will very soon end in catastrophe from the planning of tyrants, dictators, and terrorists who thought that they were blessed by their god to be like gods. They have combined extremism with greed and fundamentalism within their religious groups to rule as dictators!

A closely knit group of Special Operations Forces from NATO nations felt compelled to return to this place that had killed so many of our innocent civilians in bomb attacks and preplanned catastrophes made to appear like accidents. They went over to this Eastern region because this was where the extremists decided to hide, train, and plan for their next attack. This honorable band of brothers, who had remained friends over many years, decided that they had to return to this hellhole to finish the work that they planned to do. They were stopped and placed on a time-lined withdrawal, which meant that the remaining groups would be just that much weaker against the elusive "old-world" type of fighters. Politicians do not see or think the same as warriors on the battlefield or in the area of battle.

The story explains this new type of terrorist warfare that none of these allied forces had ever trained for or planned to fight. All tactics, techniques, and procedures needed to be reevaluated and practiced until Team Jaguar had their system down to perfection, and then all of our military forces had to change their Standard Operating Procedures (SOPs). Team Jaguar trained day in and day out. They cross-trained with their allied NATO partners to ensure that they were all on the same page of understanding ground fighting, radio-call procedures for call for fire and extractions, as well as all other facets of battle. As a finely tuned machine, they had many researchers and developers brainstorm and test simulated actions on the battlefield. Special warfare and the way of protecting our nation along with our allied friends had changed since they had retired. In this story, we will learn more of their plan and how this team of hardened warriors would conduct their attack to simulate a natural disaster!

The misinterpretation of the Muslims' holy book, the Koran, has led to the decline of Islam throughout the world. Its leaders constantly schemed new ways to create chaos around the world so they could rule by fear. This went on for many centuries and through many empires. The primary question that is difficult, if not impossible to understand is, "who are the good Muslims/Islamists from the extremist terrorist groups that have mis-interpreted the Koran to be peaceful and loving people. Then another verse says," to kill anyone that does not follow the beliefs" This can all be found online by searching the internet for Koran.

The main religion, before it was partially turned into fundamentalist ideology, reflected a belief in God, just not a Christian God. Muslims also do not use the Holy Bible as Christians do. They do believe in Jesus Christ, however. Mohammed and Allah are their versions of our Jesus story and walking with the Lord. The book that they follow is the Koran, which has scriptures similar to those of our Bible; they follow some of these scriptures or writings as law. Those who do not follow the Koran or its religious ideologies are considered as treasonous outsiders. Extremists claim the book teaches them to kill or cause chaos, mostly for the western world and its allies, especially America, but basically for all those who do not follow their beliefs.

The Bible states that God will shake the earth because there is so much disobedience from his guidance and direction as given to us in the Biblical scriptures. The separation of church and state causes politicians to try to control nations and pass laws that are contradictory with how God planned our lives to be. In a world with so much division, political scandal, conspiracies, and crime, something needs to be fixed! Consequences come to solutions for resolving the issues.

Islam and Muslim fundamentalists try to spread their socialistic beliefs in governing nations, and terror is on the rise. The most powerful and free nation in the world is now on the verge of collapse—due to a failed government and leadership that was questionably Muslim. The United States selected as its president one who many believed would be the first multiethnic man in history to be a president. Many voters felt it was not politically correct to use his black skin color or foreign descent or judge his religion as factors when deciding their vote. Not having any prior military service should have been the primary indicator that this constituent was not experienced enough to handle a global super-power nation or international affairs. Outside of the Muslim nations anyway?

Many citizens of this great western superpower nation had become too comfortable with their freedoms, even after being attacked by a terrorist group from the Arab world on our World Trade Center in New York City. This was like another Pearl Harbor strike only the enemy was scattered and hidden. They used sleeper cells that had grown up as someone's neighbor, coworker, or kids who played together. This terror cell had orders to hijack our own aircraft and crash them into national icons and facilities of federal government importance. By using these planes filled with fuel as the explosive for their missiles, they could create the most damage, death, and chaos to our nation! A strong response was necessary in demonstrating that we are a nation not to be tested or attacked without consequences.

I can remember in my younger years serving in our military; the pride and respect that other nations had for us was what honor feels like. This has slowly diminished and is growing ever weaker under this supposed leaderless administration that is in place now. After the terrorist attacks in 2001, we had an honorable yet humble and strong leader as our president. He had our military and allied forces hunt down the terrorists and place restrictions on nations that supported or sponsored terror. Such nations received the worst sanctions, but there is still much work that has been left undone.

This new, weaker leader has placed a deadline on our war against terror and allows the "media terrorist intelligence networks" to advise the world of our intentions, which only emboldens the enemies to pull back and regroup so they can later return in full force. A compromise to plans that had already been emplaced to defeat this threat! The peace we were able to restore to our nation and her people, the terrorists would ruin. Think of all the blood our brothers spilled for a compromised leadership in the west! We will not allow this or the nuclear threat to remain! National leaders will change, but this threat will always remain unless it is taken care of by professionals who know and understand how to orchestrate this takedown.

As another slap in the face, another terrorist group attached to them all planned 9/11 types of reunion. They began to protest in the streets outside of an American Embassy in Benghazi, Libya. Then, as darkness fell on the region, these terrorists staged a violent attack using RPGs, mortar fire, and machine guns to massacre the Ambassador and three other American personnel. As messages were transmitted to the administration requesting more assistance, the standards of operations (SOPs) were not followed and no assistance was ordered to rescue our own people. Was this a conspiracy or a cover-up? Weeks went by with the left-wing media talking about some anti-Muslim video that caused this riot. Muslims can burn, spit, and stomp on our flag, and nothing is said by the members of this C&C (conspiracy and cover-up).

Now it is our turn to demonstrate that we are not just sleeping, and we cannot be taken so easily. We may have been compromised to a point, but we have also identified this compromise and pledged to seek out, detect, and extinguish any threats to the free world! We now say to the terrorists, "You can run, but you cannot hide forever. We will hunt you and find you!" With the newest and smartest technology systems will find and locate you if you have bad intentions or evil thoughts. Here it comes.

There are many nations or regions in the world that throughout history have conducted illegal activities. Researching history can teach many things about a region. A small percentage of the followers of these religions have followed orders from terrorist leaders and have been involved with the laborious work to create an underground infrastructure where people will be able to survive for long periods of time. In addition, they can transport supplies and terrorists around and into other countries through tunnel networks that have been worked on for centuries! Thus, the terrorists can conduct cross-border manipulation. All of this is in preparation for the day when the psychotic jihad leaders think that they can take control of the world.

Only after several insidious and horrendous attacks around the world, which killed hundreds of thousands of innocent civilians, does it become evident where the powder keg is hidden. At that point, some very brave men from a joint group of allied nations will react to this war that has been launched against us and end the evil once and for all! A nuke could have prevented these wars, but using a nuke would not have been approved by this leader. There would have been collateral damage, but that happens in any war. These terrorists kill themselves more than would die in any military combat! Their supreme jihadist leader has been terminated, along with many in the chain of command! Yet like cockroaches, they evolve and reassemble themselves to coordinate efforts to grow and protect their nest.

This, no doubt, comes from the history of the Arab nations, controlled mostly by Iran, Persia was then overrun by fanatical Islamic fundamentalism Iran brought barbaric laws and torture to the people and oppressed the people with these laws.

Spiritual warfare started from the very beginning of time on this earth. 'Good vs. evil!'

This might possibly have followed an order from the heavens to shake the earth.

From some two thousand years ago when Jesus walked in Israel to now, so many things have changed, both good and evil. There seems to be more darkness than light these days. There are so many similarities between the holy books of these religions, yet there is a clear message of good versus evil that differs between them!

Israel is caught between the Islam nations, which all want to take the land that belongs to the Jews and wipe out Israel altogether.

Vulnerabilities are shared by all and are the same in this situation. The media and religion have opened the deepest secrets of the hidden rivalries. Looking at a map of the Middle East, it becomes clear just how weapons and terrorist soldiers are moved in and out in plain sight. The free world is compromised by Muslim fanatics who move into the free world acting out charades in order to fit in like loyal citizens in that nation!

The timed fuse starts in the West in North America and detonates in the Eastern Asia area. One can be pushed and challenged for only so long. Then a move has to be decided on, as well as the time when the move will be made. The way this world in general reacts to change and the loss of quality and appreciation for human life has lowered the standard. Why can we not have peace and just respect one another? There are no common manners or courtesies anymore, and some people think that they are above God. The situation is out of control!

The planet is even beginning to show signs of anger, with disastrous natural storms and seismic activities in many of the world's active volcanic regions.

Just as with wars and tactics used in the past, hostage taking and assassinations are being used by these terrorist groups. They even use chemical gases to kill protestors among their own people!

Researching the lessons learned from historical field commanders' after-action reports (AARs) can teach a lot about the enemies' methods of operation (MO). To catch a terrorist, you must think like a terrorist! This is what B. B., the intel guy, would say to the paramilitary group of seasoned veterans. And it is true! (B. B. was an intelligence representative for the US Army, an E-7, for fourteen or so years. He has a wife and a five-year-old daughter at his home in the suburbs of upper New York. He got sick of watching the national leadership, which was caught up in so many controversial issues that seemed un-American and left the army due to lack of faith and trust in the leadership.)

As noted above, terrorist units can travel underground through the tunnel networks without detection. They can time their attacks, video the fights, and stage scenarios to give civilized nations a black eye through the use of media news stories and the terrorists' filming of the activities. They are skilled at using these dis-information and advertising tools. Confidentiality right on the news! The media was the main intelligence source for what was happening in certain key areas of the world and also provided target points for planning. The media could help terrorists develop plans from daily updates from incidents, catastrophes, political events, and financial standing, while also providing global advertising of their groups' strength and accountability for certain attacks, bombings, and other activities.

The deception game among rival nations was in full operation, compromising the world and disclosing future strategies for total control. Vulnerabilities were often televised and discussed in the open by the media. Secret and personal information passed in televised broadcast news that could endanger our military operations and international affairs from divulging information solely meant for this nation. Yet the news is televised internationally, so this can compromise particular events or activities on going or planned for in the near future. Team Jaguar has some military friends that are still in this Area of Operations in the Middle East. They can drop our initial probes close to the cave openings that lead to the Islamic National Highway, INH. This will provide them with the necessary soil and sample rock make up in order to develop their sensors and explosives covered camouflage. Once the team retrieves the information from the sensors, they can remotely be destructed to dust.

More and more, the governments of the world began practicing the theory of following a supreme leader and conducting closed-doors negotiations on how citizens' lives and the nation would be controlled. In some nations, this secrecy really wasn't noticed because that was the norm in their lives. Socialist nations did not recognize the deceptive and secretive changes to tax codes, their failing economies, and fewer jobs for the people. People's rights were almost nonexistent, and this started complete chaos and an explosion of anger and distrust in the streets of many nations! As the people realized that their personal retirement accounts were locked down and that the personal health and entitlements would be less each month or quarter, that they were nationally dependent on what their nation's leadership was doing and the deals that were being made, the world was falling into a chaotic situation.

In the free Democratic nations, people really began to get angry, and more control was placed upon them. The conspiracies with national governments and their use of the terror groups to help them accomplish this new world of supreme control were not completely identified until there was a clear season of bombings and attacks. "Embassies ransacked and ambassadors with security murdered by the 'peaceful' Muslim Extremists! Veteran's groups shot up and attacks on schools, shopping malls, and so on!" And the clock keeps ticking! Public events, Embassy infrastructure and personnel! More consequences to fall by.

The primary concern is to protect Israel from all of the surrounding Muslim Brotherhood extremist nations that wish to attack them with a weapon of mass destruction or a nuke from one of the extremist nations or from the head of the snake itself, Iran. The terrorists can get away with burning national flags of western nations and allies of Israel, and we are told not to retaliate by this anus sitting in my president's seat! Everyone who is loyal and intelligent wants this idiot gone! The ignorant, undereducated blacks and others like him because he can speak well. He does not appear to be empowered to help with fixing our nation's financial debt or economy, but he sure likes to spend our money! So much that military cuts are turning member's rogue! Similarities with our friendly nations have also been seen!

It is time for change in many ways! There has been an uprising of domestic violence and terrorism in many nations as well. Some psycho breaks into a small children's school and shoots almost two dozen innocent little kids and teachers. What is going on here?

Everyone must be more vigilant to notice those who do not act normally or have a lot of anger. People must learn to speak up and report things that do not appear correct. A man walks into a shopping mall with a rifle. This is not normal, and anyone could have called the police or jumped on him to prevent the shooting that occurred.

Instead, disasters were put on a board and analyzed by sequential dates, calamities, and national situations with elections or some form of new laws to give more power to these corrupt leaders and co-conspirators. There is an aimpoint on their heads.

Jobs are on the decline and more families are struggling to make ends meet and survive, while the fat cats live a rich life and never have the concerns of the working-class citizens. Watching our young warriors come back in caskets and hearing the stories of heroism and valor made us all proud of our heritage when we were young. But now we all have set the foundations for these similar attacks and been part of their training cadre. An Army Colonel flips out in a shooting range and kills some of his own units' men. And this Colonel was Arabic. Could this have been a pre-planned attack by provided orders from the Muslim Brotherhood? These are a group of Arab extremists that will soon be terminated by something that has never been seen or experienced in world history. Instead, the government media puts out that "this was a lone gunman and a confined event"? "My butt". 'Propaganda!'

This was starting to affect everyone! Then the simple, random attacks that would kill and wound a few innocent civilians began to catch our attention. We were told stories in our earlier years about these sleeper cells that would come to our nation and become nationalized citizens with multiple citizenships and passports. They could travel freely and target the special called-upon targets to gather information on them and then fly back to whichever nation they were training in and pass the information to the cell leader? All this went totally under the radar and unnoticed! All because of the PC (Politically Correct) Syndrome. Captain Morgan stated, "This information is now stored in an international terrorist data base computer and red –flagged on their every move. By facial recognition, DNA and ethnicity special sensor satellites are providing NATO and necessary criminal justice systems with every aspect of these extremists and the holes that they hide in. This is where the miniature combat vehicles will be of great service for the locating and termination of this international and evil threat to society.

Immigration is the starting point of data collection for intelligence collections for keeping the nation entered safe from a potential threat. These potentials can be tracked by the local intelligence networks to maintain watch and security countermeasures if necessary.

The media would stand up for terrorists if one was killed or captured, but not for one of our own citizens! It breaks our laws, and so on. G.W.O.T. Idiot! That is what they declared us by blowing up our World Trade Center Towers on September 11, 2001! That is enough justification for me when they killed thousands of innocent people so harshly by flying passenger airliners into them! If someone from Team Jaguar were in charge, each one of these terrorists would suffer a fierce and nasty death! With so much unimaginable pain, they should have been wiped out for doing this!

Their time will come faster than they could imagine. The entire Jihad Crusade Conspiracy will soon be compromised, all the traitors living within the Global Alliance of Nations will be compromised, and the entire plan will be blown apart. All this terror and damage, because of some selfishly power-hungry idiots. The Muslim Brotherhood is an allegiance to a psychopathic ideology of extremism that could watch their fellow citizens and human beings starve, die, or become impoverished from a broken economy and lack of jobs because of these greedy SOBs!

With our Holy Land surrounded by these enemy extremists, the most powerful nation in the world will be the lead in bringing this evil, terrible regime down! Along with our friendly allied nations, we can do this! We must do this. We are close to certain on the people within our nation who have compromised our government, the financial sector, and the judicial system to work with them. Probably from under-the-table payoffs and promises of some dark type. Every day we are getting closer, and fraudulent information is being identified. "To protect our nation from all enemies, foreign or domestic"! And that we will. So, yes, we are very close, and a huge conspiracy it is, beyond anything ever imagined! Cover-ups, scandals, and crimes of the highest against their own nation's constitutional laws and service member's lives 'Jihadist sympathizer's will be included to the target list as well!'.

There must be hundreds who have died in vain, all for some scandalous political agenda of a cowardly and spineless wannabe ruler. C. C. was not considered to mean commander and chief anymore. It was campaigner and celebrity! Because he was more interested in the Hollywood types and getting in as many photo opportunities as possible when campaigning! And then there are consequences for all wrong's to be corrected. ROMANS 13:4 For he is GOD's minister to thee, for good. But if thou do that which is Evil, fear: for he beareth not the sword in vain, for he is GOD's minister: an avenger to execute wrath upon him that doth evil.

Introduction to the Main Characters: Team Jaguar

All of these men are highly educated, from university graduates to PhDs. Each also has his unique skill set to blend into and offer this mission. They are all highly nonexpendable! Each member of this team is cross trained to understand and operate in another's position if necessary. The team is split into two different areas, for secrecy, as split elements of the combined team, and can function as one unit if desired.

1. Morgan: The mission leader and best-known in this global community of warriors. A former USN SEAL captain named Jack went by Captain Morgan for his nickname. A strong and capable leader who can think out of the box. He understood the word betrayal all too well from being retired from a "Heightened Defense-joint position" within the Washington DC functions and operations. He saw something that was wrong and spoke up to try and correct it. Being too close to the political election cycle, this first-term president had a very suspicious background and history. The president betrayed him and tried to have him shut up for good. Morgan decided to exit the theater and then caught some word from key Jaguar players within the team who are close with him. He was easily selected to join and then to lead the team. His experience in this area of operations (AO) is second to none. He has operated in this area for more than ten years of his twenty-six-year career. Working in the intelligence community of the DC area really helped a lot with knowledge of the area.

2. Pete: Morgan's second-in-command and the commanding officer of site #2. retired eloquently after being screwed by the DC bureaucrats. He was about to transfer to a higher-level combatant

command, and they wanted him to take a lower position, so he left. He is one hell of an operator and all-around nice guy! He would literally give you the shirt off his back if you needed it. Triathlete and water sports guy, he loved the jungles of South America and had deployed around the world on numerous combat missions. Skilled helicopter pilot and UAV controller.

3. Duke: The Dane, as they called him. He came from a legendary history of warriors back to the Viking clan days. He is a highly intelligent man, six feet tall, with a bald head and Fu-Manchu goatee mustache, strong and husky. He has a PhD in psychology and speaks four languages fluently: Norwegian, English, Spanish, and Arabic. Avery well-decorated combat veteran, with some scars from injuries to prove it!

4. Doc: His real name is Jesse, but he is used to being called Doc, mainly because he was a combat medic in the trauma tent! As a highly skilled physician as well as a warrior, he was getting bored with his private service.

5. Joey: A talented technician and engineer. He worked with the USN Seabees in the engineering department, which was also attached to the Special Operations Forces (SOF), mostly with the SEALS-deploying squadrons. He would assist with the facility setup and development, and then oversee that all the specialized communication links were all set up and functioning properly.

6. B. B.: was an explosives ordnance disposal (EOD) technician, and Sensor/UAV controller/repairman. He is a medium build, straight to the point type of guy with a sense of humor. He can play the Harmonica like a pro, and entertains the team when not on a workstation.

7. Shit-Bag: His real name is A. J. He was in a serious auto accident during a return trip home from a mission. An oncoming truck swerved into his lane, and they had a head-on collision. He came close to dying, but after multiple surgeries, he was able to pull through. The only thing was that his internal organs had been so messed up that the

doctors had to take out his colon and give him a colostomy bag to defecate into. With humor, he was given the nickname, 'Shitbag! He could and did still operate for years after that. He got out after fifteen years of service to attend college and be a civilian. He is another of the technicians in the team. He is the IT wizard, and imaging is his specialty. Employed as a NASA technician, he assisted with many exploratory visual aids and is a visual-screen genius.

8. Tommy: Intel Tommy was a retired USA Sgt. Major, SOF Intelligence Operator and Public Affairs Officer for media BS! He is also a great sniper and can prep a deer faster than Jethro can BBQ a burger.

9. Tony: A big war dog retired SOF, Green Beret, he had been on missions with all of us and was an all-hands-on kind of guy. Experienced with everything, just an all-natural fix it man. Married to a strong and understanding woman, with two beautiful little daughters.

10. Billy.: A US Army SOF Paratrooper. He is married and has a five-year-old son. He is a recon and surveillance (R&S) expert and was a tunnel rat for his active-duty patrols. He can repair any camera or night-vision equipment just as fast as any member can field-strip and put back together their rifles. Half of his right leg is prosthetic from staging a booby trap in a tunnel complex. Counter surveillance and signal jamming are his specialties.

11. Dex: Another cock-strong bull triathlete type that likes to do R&S. He has a wife and two children, one boy and one girl. They are in their early teens. He is an avid run, swim, bike, and kayak type of guy. He had a desire to work in criminal justice and had a master's degree in the field. He lost interest after seeing too many conspiracies and dirty, corrupt lawyers and judges playing with people's lives, both in releasing guilty criminals and incarcerating innocent people! How can people get away with destroying other's lives? God will have the final say!

12. Troy: One of the Nordics within the team, with a legendary background from the Viking warrior days! A Swedish native, he moved to the United States as a teenager and joined the military. He stands six foot two inches, with blond hair and a short mustache. A

master at Kung Fu and other fighting arts, this man could walk into an enemy patrol and walk out alive, with nothing more than a small cut or bruise, with blood on his clothes but not his own. He would always sing old Nordic songs when drinking. He also had an old helmet with the mountain goat horn sticking up on it. Predator told him that he would like that or even buy it from him if we all made it out of this Shiite-hole. He has a deep robust laugh. Like the other Nordic warrior from the Danes, he offers us much as far as both land- and sea-fighting techniques. He is an explosives ordnance technician and chemist. He could make explosives from things that no one else would ever have thought was possible.

13. George: Probably the only real civilian physicist with the team. He was the geologist/scientist who would help to detect the various particles and elements that are associated with chemical, biological, radiological, and nuclear (CBRN) types of weapons, or WMD. It took a week to completely get his lab set up and all the high-tech machines blinking and flashing away. No one else really understood all of what this equipment did, except for some of the other techies who may have had some prior experience in school or training with them.

14: Al: A Vietnam Era SEAL A big brother type. He had finished his second career with S.W.A.T. He was known for his aggressive actions and had made himself into an all-round ground fighter. With his mixed bag of experience from the martial arts (Kung Fu, Jit Kun Do, and cage fighting), he was not one to be messed with.

15. Predator is the shadow coordination team manager. His unprecedented experience has resulted in closed-loop connections with highly secretive and wealthy contributors who would like the chance to make things right again—or as close as could be for a peaceful life! The donors have generously outfitted the team with enough secret cash to move a mountain or buy an island with. Predator understands just what it takes to get an enemy nation's civilians to cross over to provide human intelligence and aid where needed. They live in such poverty that they help us to earn some extra, secret money that can provide for their families.

16. T-Bone: Is a tall handsome and brut looking operator on the team. He is a great operator and a technology genius.

• Stephan, Chuck, Robbie and some other players are part-time players and covert support for the team when called in for their help. Steve also operated as the site 2 X.O. for Pete, or second in command. Executive Officer.

The financial assistance from those secretive supporters is very much appreciated, and the team will do their best to make all of you quietly proud!

Each team site could function with complete unity as one or separately if something were to malfunction on one site. Each site resembled the other and had half of the team at each site (like an element) to function and operate the equipment as required There are some other shadow warrior assistants that can be called on at any time for temporary operations. Chuck is one of these extra experts and friend to the team.

Each site also had a shadow contingent of two scientists, a chemist and a biologist, to determine the contagions that might be found by the sensor devices; as well as two intelligence technicians (ITs) to help assemble the sensor monitoring and communications systems.

These sixteen + highly skilled warriors are on standby for now. The additional members, scientists or technicians will be brought in when needed; under deep cover to not compromise each site position of this split team.

The team has many operatives assisting with coordination of assets and supplies needed for the team. All these shadow members are managed by Predator.

When the order comes to move or initiate, they will be on the move executing this operation like it had been rehearsed over a hundred times. There are many other shadow operators who provide assistance quietly. All sixteen are married to the toughest and most understanding women on the planet, who deal with the separation plus not knowing what could happen and about the safety of their husbands.

Even though there are many in the Special Forces from many different units, they are a Force of One!

<u>**Acronyms**</u>

(G.W.O.T). Global War On Terror!

(A.O). Area Of Operations.

(ISR), Intelligence, Surveillance, Reconnaissance

CBRN: Chemical, Biological, Radiological, and Nuclear weapons

CS: Counter surveillance

C4ISR: Acronym for Command, Control, Communications and Computers-Intelligence, Surveillance, Reconnaissance.

Element: Is a part or smaller section of a larger unit or team. A sub- unit of the main body.

EOD: Explosive Ordnance Disposal

IED: Improvised Explosive Device

INH: Islamic National Highway

NSW: Naval Special Warfare

R&S: Reconnaissance and Surveillance

RDT&E: Research, Development, Test, and Evaluation

SOCOM: Special Operations Command

SOF: Special Operations Forces

WMD: Weapons of Mass Destruction

References

The fuse and powder keg drawings were hand-sketched to simulate split continents. The directional bezel was hand-drawn from an image found on any map, world atlas, or navigational compass. All sketches and geological fault lines, INH, are from the author's imagination.

Drone Introductions

The introduction to the miniaturized, unmanned aerial vehicles (UAVs) and ground vehicles (drones). All of these are realistic-looking and high-technology machines that can be the eyes, ears, and noses for Team Jaguar. The team does utilize a standard UAV also for C4ISR data collection.

The UAV/Drones are used for the ISR needed by the team to collect and analyze this vital information. Any miniaturized drones not shown are still under test and production for this mission and others to defeat those who decide to cross the line and threaten the United States and our interests. Some of these ISR systems have not been printed. A flat bed wrecker tow truck that is miniaturized and made like a remote controlled "Tonka" truck reinforced chassis and body to move around the equipment and explosive devices that will be utilized by team Jaguar to complete their mission and destroy the Extremist groups underground routes and weapons caches. This is not shown but a highly used piece of our high-tech inventory of combat platforms.

• Some combat miniature Drones are not able to be displayed at this time, due to classification status and testing.

Flies:

Mosquito:

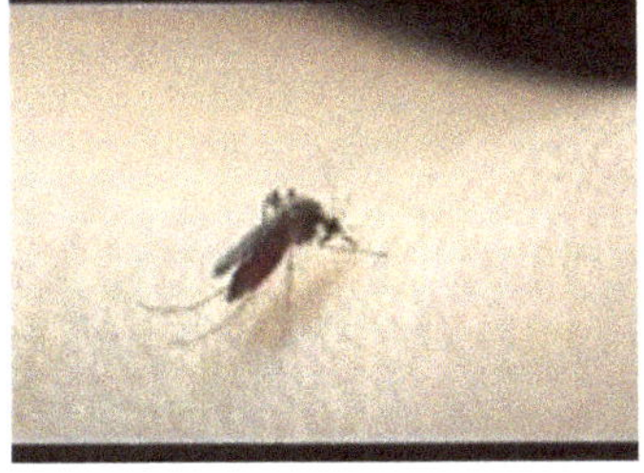

Bat:

Ground Combat ISR Drones: Ant, Fly, Mosquitoe,Bat.

The explosive packages that Team Jaguar will use to complete their mission are a high fusion hydrogen/nuclear device camouflaged to look like a common rock as seen in this area of operation/A.O. An 80-pound explosive charge encased into a hard plastic. This plastic is specially textured and colored to appear like an ordinary rock. They are acoustically detonated from the sound waves that come from the previous detonation down and along this train of explosives. The team has several ways to have these charges delivered and placed or released at the area in which this particular charge will have coverage. It is difficult to understand, but there are so many ignorant people unaware that there is this threat or that we are at war. They live their daily lives like a social recluse that is ignorant and does not have the ability to mentally comprehend issues that they dislike or that could interfere with their daily way of living. Their normal comfort zone. So strong Patriots must take the stand and fight to protect what freedoms we do have and our citizens.

Some of the drones, such as the spider drone are still being tested and could not be published at this time. They will participate in the mission
to assist team Jaguar.

Chapter One
Out of Retirement

(Predator narrates the story about team Jaguar). Many career military warriors, when it comes time to call it quits and retire after twenty years or more served in some of the most arduous conditions, stressful on the body as well as the mind, need some decompression time relaxing with family and friends. Some even want to be alone during this decompression time. They often want to live in peace in a mountain cabin near a stream for fishing, with land to provide wild game. They want fresh air and the sound of a light breeze in the trees or a casual bird call. I can remember every evening at dusk, old Woody the Woodpecker would start pecking. Tap, tap, tap, and tap. And after a short break, he would repeat it.

Then you start to think about who you are and all the adventurous things and dangerous but fun things as well that you did! Then you start missing the old times with buddies and worldly travels. Then the dreams begin to wake you at night in a sweat.

The Special Operations Forces (SOF) is a very tight-knit group of masters of many war-fighter skills. Everyone goes through a period of time either really grieving the loss of close teammates or from not being with the unit wherever they may have been deployed to for training or on a real mission. Some days, Predator would sit on a tree stump and practice his knife and hatchet throwing at some mock-up targets that he had built from wood, cardboard and straw, hay, old clothes, and so on; these materials were used for stuffing the targets for the fullness necessary to hold the weapons as a real flesh body would if stuck with a knife or hatchet. He had a small blanket with six perfectly balanced throwing knives. They were sharp too! He had cut himself many times practicing, just as did other guys who had learned this art. You learn not to hold them too tightly, and to hold the flat part away from the sharp edges. When throwing, it is a smooth gentle loosening of the grip and release when the wrist is pointed directly at the point of impact that leads to success. If the knife is held too tight, there is a much greater chance of getting cut, missing the target, or both.

It did not take long to come together with a plan that would prepare and train these warriors for the mission and get their physical fitness standards back to what would be needed to pull off this mission.

They had to stop shaving their beards immediately to blend in with the locals.

Next would be to rotate who would plan and run the fitness training. Doc would run the daily medical training and scenarios.

Stephan was a combat helicopter pilot and had his own for play also. He was the number 2 in command for site# 2, and Pete's Executive Officer. Able to take control if Pete was engaged in something else of importance. He would ensure that our emergency support would be ready when we went in and could assist with some of the training. We had some very close contacts in the governments and military that could provide some of the military hardware that would be necessary for the job to be pulled off successfully and give the appearance of a natural disaster or accident by the terrorists in a weapons cache in the mountains or tunnel network between borders.

Finances were provided by very wealthy funders who were not very happy with the global situation, not to mention the people who'd made it into powerful places by smooth talk and BS. We were also provided with a safe account for each member's retirement that could not be touched.

In the meantime, Dex, Joey, and B. B. began playing with some new surveillance equipment. They were top-of-the-line point men with all kinds of sensors—sensors for explosives, booby traps, other counter surveillance jamming equipment remote-controlled by the operator with grabbers and 4x4s for rugged movement and UAVs. They also oversaw recorders to send information forward or for reach-back capabilities for ground commanders. This newest technology was like being in the comfort of a recliner chair and playing a video game with a friend or kid. It is amazing what a brilliant mind can think up!

For a test run of one of the unmanned aerial vehicles or drones, this particular one had an arm to grab a rock or soil sample. From the rock collections, the scientists could reproduce sample IED rocks that blended in with the terrain and ground sensors for video and noise feedback; they could even be detonated like a fragmentation grenade if some curious raghead wanted to see it closer.

B. B., the explosives expert, was preparing some classes for the team on new weapons and explosives technology that was supplied to us by some very gracious and generous supporters and manufacturers. The most important and impressive demolitions device was part nuclear and part hydrogen fission in a man pack nuke basically. It just had more power than usual and was not yet released to public knowledge, which made it even better to disguise the cause of the attack. Special weapons systems designed for Special Operations Forces are to be the designed and separated at the distance that will cause this chain reaction of acoustically detonated devices to create the impression of a natural disaster in the form of an earthquake. We were even thinking of using some of the chemical-biological agents used by Saddam, and located underground after a close explosives cache had detonated and opened a side of a small hill where they were found and identified and then passed to us to hide for safekeeping.

We, of course, kept some for our own surprise use on a terrorist network underground. This would put the fear of Allah into them and provide a short distracter for the team's movement and placement of traps and surprises for our mole friends there. While they were in chaos watching their flesh melt from each other's bodies, the team could be completing more tasks without interruption. This would secure them during extraction from the patrol and placement of the fuse chain. Left behind in their tracks were surprises and more surprises for any enemy units trying to pursue the team's plan. Getting down into the tunnel network was the most fascinating. You actually felt like you were there, but you were in the control center, viewing a video screen while smoking a cigar and drinking a rum and coke or whatever beverage.

The underlying motivation for these men is their faith in Christianity and Jesus Christ, being warriors for his sacrifice and the cause for all the others who are oblivious to this jihad (holy war, which these Muslim fanatics have been planning  to do to the world). The warriors of our God/ Jesus would do the work needed to preserve all Christianity should the Lord not act on time because we know that Jesus would not want anything this atrocious to happen to his people. Psalm 23 ("As I walk through the shadow of the Valley of death"), which every one of this team's members had, provides more motivation to justify this mission in remembrance of our fallen warriors. Some had fallen to improvised explosive devices (IEDs) that had been set as a booby trap to ambush troop movement or simply left in a place that these rags knew there might be a US or any enemy patrol on their land. In a large population there are many that will not and only a choice few that will, these are the "warriors".

All of this information and planning was shared with both of the teams' sites. This was to ensure that everyone was on the same page and understood the ideas and methodology for carrying out the mission. Each of the members that had a SOF background understood what the (EOD)Explosives Ordnance Disposal guy was explaining.

The team would all get together during planning phases for a short prayer and to ask for guidance and forgiveness if this was not meant to happen this way.

"The ultimate sacrifice", is when a soldier lays down his/her life for the safety of the fellow members and to defeat the enemy forces.

As dark as the world was looking, many Christians began to wonder if the end was near.

Living a life in total compromise that the average regular civilian would think is only political disagreements? Compromise is something completely different, and if nothing is not done soon about this, then the world will be ruled by our enemies and all of the conspirators that join them. The African black Muslim majority and NAACP have learned how to blend right into rapper society and the hip-hop, rap influences. Many terror groups are from the African Cape, all black in skin color, and are from Yemen, Egypt, and other nations. They are all the tribes, African Panthers, and so on that are all involved for the money part with Al-Qaeda and other splinter groups from the African nations. They used to be friendly to westerners and outsiders, until they joined forces with terror groups that paid more and gave a clan more for a few suicide/homicidal vest bombers. It started in the Arab and European nations mostly as a training environment. Russia had a few hits to try and make the world think that they had no involvement or influence. The main objective was to get control of as many nuclear nations as possible. The quotes from the Holy Christian Bible section of the Revelations and Rapture make understandable the part about the burning of the surface of the earth. The Arab world is ready to explode (literally), and one nation is leading this revolution or brotherhood jihad. That is what will be taken out and is the end of the time fuse!

Israel constantly has to be on guard and alert because of the Iranian-led terror groups that spread around into other nations to surround the small nation of Israel. Iran was continuing to get their hands on nuclear weapons. The Muslim Brotherhood was a planned combining or forced persuasion to join with all of the Arab nations or Islam. That would destabilize the entire region, and even neighboring nations were not comfortable with this bringing global attention and scrutiny by the nations for them to seize and stop causing international waves. Everyone knew that these extremist groups would use these weapons on their key enemy only because of religious history and a superpower nation of Christian heritage and founding. This could bring on the Apocalypse if these extremists kept pushing other nation's buttons. It would mean complete and total obliteration of them if they were to attack Israel or these other nations using some form of nuclear weapon. This region is sitting on top of a powder keg.

The weekly News propaganda only expedited the planning and preparations to deploy this operation. Was this holy joining for peace? They called it "Arab spring," which in reality was the combining of force to fulfill extremist ideology and psychopathic mythology about the taking over of the world. If sanctions are placed on these government's trade and imports, then  innocent civilians will suffer. The leaders are all certain that their families will all eat and not go hungry. Some of these extremist nations are talking about using chemical gas or toxin weapons on their own people who protest/demonstrate against poor living conditions.

The time to move was coming sooner than they expected. But from news sources, it was not a shock to the team and supporting members that the time to react had come early. A Muslim nation falling to a new election and a member of the "Muslim Brotherhood" placing himself as the new president caused much alarm around the world. Being a partial barrier for the Holy Land, the west sent over a negotiator to assure that peace was the main agenda. They supposedly came to a satisfactory agreement. Then the next day this newly self-proclaimed leader then gave himself complete and total rule even above their Supreme Court. He also fired the highest-ranking remaining military leadership and replaced them with his M-B personnel. So much for democracy and a peaceful agreement! Another dictator threatens to use chemical weapons on his own people for protesting about the lack of food and medicines for their families, as well as poor healthcare treatment. Consequences mount with global tension on this situation.

The guys in the team would occasionally speak with their families and loved ones using the encrypted SATCOM radio set. They could not say much because of the highly sensitive classified mission they were planning. Even the key national leaders could not know of this. There was great suspicion that the governments of many of the allied nations had been infiltrated, though it could not be said at what level or how high, though a couple of the leaders were even suspect. When daily activity is surrounded by deception such as this, it can be difficult to sleep with all that knowledge in your mind—but never to fail, a few

drinks of rum, whiskey, or beer could help relax them enough to sleep. A good day of work completed!

More intelligence and imagery came in from the miniature drones (bats, flies, etc.) that had been sent out on a short R&S mission. They had located a very secure bunker of some type, and about 100 kilometers down from the surface, there was an escape or entry tunnel, implying that there might be some possible prisoners locked in a small chamber. The image was dark, and there was not sufficient illumination for the night vision to show a better picture. This would need to be revisited the next day or soon. Once identified, the entrance would be marked, and there would be a TS, (Top – Secret) message sent to SOF to take action ASAP. They would need to send in a squad or some element to physically extract those

prisoners if that is what they are. Interpol and the NATO SOF would have to determine that.

The clock was the enemy at this point for the planning, and just knowing that the enemy had more time to plan out their own strategies for attacks on Christianity could make your nerves unsettled. The Islamic religion was suspect in this global war, (Jihad) that they had declared. The people who had no part of this scheme were still looked at as suspects and potential threats.

Just how far behind or in what stage was the enemy? Some of their very own nations' national security was at risk. The team knew that they could only talk with members of their active-duty teams who were friends or team members when they worked together years in the past. The message must become clear to the plan for the planet and might be located in a comparison study of the Koran and the Bible. They were indeed doing just that. Some areas in the Koran have already been identified to tell its followers to cause hate and discontent with the west and others who do not agree with their beliefs. So, claim the extremist Muslim groups? A true study is needed to both understand the enemy and to answer some questions about the Koran and its teachings. Maybe the extreme-control fanatics portrayed and deciphered the word in their own way to control the masses and force this idealism onto them. More will follow on this topic.

An example of extreme change could be of the Old Persian Empire approximately (1400 A.D) +; a thousand+ years ago. The empire was one of international trade, with peaceful people and life held in high regard. It was called the international land of trade, a peaceful, happy people trading in rugs, sweaters, blankets, perfume, ornaments, spices, perfumes and so on.

Then entered Islamic fundamentalism and barbaric rule. It is now Iran some 1500 A.D.+ years later. The Islamic National Highway (INH) was made for the general purpose of clandestine movement and kept all of their secrets from the world hidden under nearly one-mile-thick shale-stone bedrock as a fortified and impenetrable underworld city. Talk about a "black market" of underground weapons, human smuggling and drug trade! They did get control of the materials and fusion machines to develop their isotopes and plan an all-out global world takeover by placing the fear of this nuclear weapons attack into all living person's hearts and minds. Chaos soon began to erupt in Europe as people scrambled to save all that they had earned in their lives from being taken away by corrupt governments, bankers, and so on. At least that is what they wanted the media to report. The Muslim news agencies spread this report like candy to a baby! All of the main news reporters and journalists around the world fought to get their hands on what could be a Pulitzer Prize in journalism or news broadcasting. Really, WTF? More liberal media contortions of news and lies! A media story was passed to warn the population that the majority of Muslim-Brotherhood nations will soon be ruled under a strict dictatorship. If the people believe in this, then they should stay. If they do not agree, they should leave this land or become prisoners or slaves to the nation!

There will be one last warning to known civilian shepherds before the earthquake happens.

Intel Tommy and Joey were hard at work making notes and configuring a plan on how and where he would acquire or borrow these new machines to use in the job. Just like the saying, "Like a fly on a wall." Pleased with the progress so far, they now knew that the larger weight-bearing drones would be needed. They would spend some time to review the video that had been received so far from the flies, ants, and spiders that had been deployed to detect and report. They were the eyes for these operators for now. They provided real-time video feedback, sonar navigation with night-vision capabilities, and air-particle sensor identification systems. This would provide the team with a more defined understanding of air quality and

any trace CBRN locations. The night fly would need to be deployed with a mini illume particle inserted to allow the NVG system to function better and provide an improved visual on that caged cell or box.

Whatever was it and what was inside? The last flight there only received audio and shadowy imagery. It sounded like people trying to whisper and communicate quietly. Troy and the other linguists would need to listen and translate what some of the guys might not understand and to define if this person or household is friendly or not. These assets will also conduct surveillance monitoring of the homes that will need to be forewarned of the situation and to determine if the home is to hostile extremists or friendlies.

This night flight brought a new sense of where the mission stood on the time line. It might possibly delay the progress. The visual imagery that was being transmitted back was indeed human prisoners of war. It looked like a mix of possible NATO MIAs and locals. This would need to be looked at much more before they could decide on the next step. Morgan was already discussing some contingencies with Pete. They called for an all-hands meeting in the conference room fifteen minutes, "on duty personnel are exempt and can be filled in later or rewind the briefing for preview and the discussion forum for review".

They sat back for a moment and revisited their own personal combat experiences and thought about how many of their fellow warrior brothers would still be alive today if we had had this awesome ISR technology that we do today! It is an incredible thing when smart minds come together and can blend imagination with realistic combat needs to manufacture such systems as they have at hand. It all came from the minds and imaginations of great warriors.

The Intel Tonka was a mechanized vehicle platform, 4x4 and ruggedized for the terrain; it would be taking the role with the point man when entering the caves and tunnels. Along with the mechanized insect patrol, this platform was a complete intelligence-gathering surveillance  tool with IR (infrared), noise recognition, movement/explosives detection, and so on. It was almost like having an extra set of eyes and a pack mule with you. Most of the equipment that the team was receiving was from contributions from their old military units or counterterrorism offices in the governments and science laboratories. The spotting and shooting scopes were top-of-the-line in quality and clarity. The IR night-vision scopes made the gear that the guys had worked with during their active years look like something prehistoric in comparison to this high-tech equipment. These listening devices could hear a whisper from 500 meters and distinguish the language to the word. Wrapped in a covering to resemble and have the texture of a common rock these devices sat in waiting, sleep mode, until the signal was turned on for them to function. An ISR system designed to resemble an ordinary rock of the area terrain had been placed by these drones and some from earlier HUMAN, SOF Patrols that had first located these caves and tunnel networks before they had been ordered by higher authority to "stand down and return to home base"?

From this technology, the team was able to watch patrols of both enemy and friendly forces on recon missions or returning from somewhere else into cover.

They could initiate the deadly mosquito UAV drone, which can inject any toxin into the target victim and allow the team's surveillance watch/operator to observe and capture the death on film for intelligence to know exactly who or which terrorist was just exterminated.

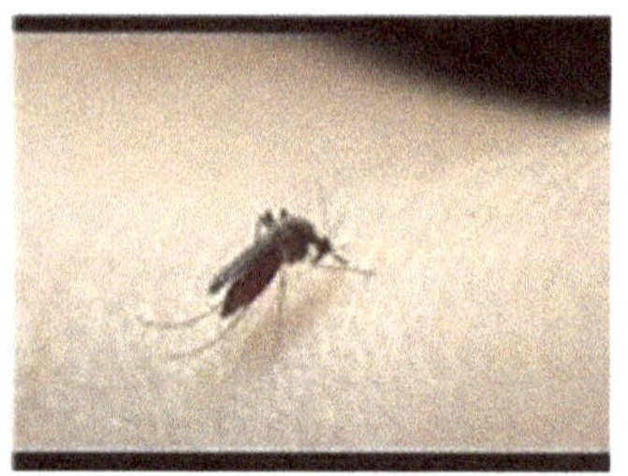

One time, the team was watching some surveillance footage of a cavern entry into the side of a mountain in the Tangier Valley of Afghanistan, when a suicide bomber accidentally blew himself up by tripping a booby trap of explosives that he was trying to set. Smoke, dust, and debris flew everywhere! One less terrorist to worry about!

Soon regular forces' foot patrols may only be necessary for specialized missions to place this new technology for future commanders to see, and for computers to control with air strikes, missile defense systems, and so on. The future holds many secrets for us to learn now that we understand the psyche of the terrorist. We know that they are everywhere and we know how and when to get them. We can determine which entry points are the most important to facilitate the delivery of the explosive packages to be placed along the fault. Time will tell. From the horn of Africa up to the northern area of Iran, this fault zigs and zags across many Arab regions. Imagine that! This will make the teams plan this much more realistic with the outcome.

As they all sat around the large conference table, they watched and listened to what the big screen monitor was showing and what Captain Morgan and Pete were telling us. The team could not believe their eyes. Could some of these prisoners be some of their own who were written off as KIA? The primary objective now would have to be to find out who these people were. "Through DNA," Jesse blurted out. As the doctor, he knew how to do this and had the technology to determine if they were any of ours from our NATO operator's medical library. He would send in five mosquitoes that had the capability to take four separate blood draws from the ten people that they had seen. The mosquito would snap a facial recognition shot and then take a blood sample. Jesse said that he could have the systems programmed and A. J. could help him set up the insect squad to be ready to deploy in fifteen minutes. In the meantime, still in their chairs viewing a split-screen, B. B. and Joey. maneuvered the mini-ant patrol farther into the crack where the nuke site was believed to be—and yes! It was there. There were the nuclear hazard warning signs in the passageway next to this room. About another 300 meters into the INH, and the crack

showed another ant had discovered a missile silo tube! This crack must be a stress fracture of some kind, maybe due to all of the construction to build this or from seismic activity over time,

We work for God and are only used to set up the meeting and judgment for the enemy earlier than expected!

Doc updated the team and Captain Morgan to relay this message if any of the team were not available to get this information. "The tests of the prisoner's that are being held in this cage have 3 American businessman, (Doctor, Journalist and one military man). There are others from the U.K; and Germany to include a n Indian national". This would need to be cleared out before the primary objective of destroying this network of deception is completed. Some of the team that are actively engaged in the operation of some of these systems are required to maintain control of their workspace and have permission to be informed when their duties are completed, or a new operator relieves them from the shift that they were working. This is the reason that the entire team and assistant operatives maintain the abilities to understand and share the duties or change positions or the control of a different drone system.

Maybe it was how these nations just blatantly spit on our legal system, which had been agreed upon after World War II by all of the nations to follow. Maybe the televised brutal murders of prisoners and their own people, or the burning of the US flag and those of other nations, was what sickened them to the point of leaving our families and friends, leaving their comfortable lives. Of course, it also could have been hearing about crime and, even worse, how the politicians were dragging the entire working class over hot coals while they lived in their cushy little world. A speech or a media promotion showed it every now and then. Too many vacations and not enough work in leadership.

It seemed like even though our laws and customs had evolved to being somewhat more civilized with the time, the leadership was still very much as if there were a monarchy and army to squelch any unrest or uprisings against the supreme leadership. Like serfs and the royals. It made us all sick with everything that we all had done and seen to protect our people from the enemy. They were already here anyway, living right in front of us. Just waiting and manipulating the laws of the land. A new dual citizen that was considered to be a frequent flier and potential spy against our nation would now be held in an international computer database that could alert the 'United Nations' security agencies of their movement or arrival. This will aide in the surveillance of possible or known terrorists now in our nation. Tracking and surveillance would take authorities directly to these terrorists safe house and possibly compromise the entire cell and leaders?

An update came onto one of the smaller visual screens; apparently one of the UAV flies had just located an underground canal or stream that connected both water sources on the Arabian Peninsula.

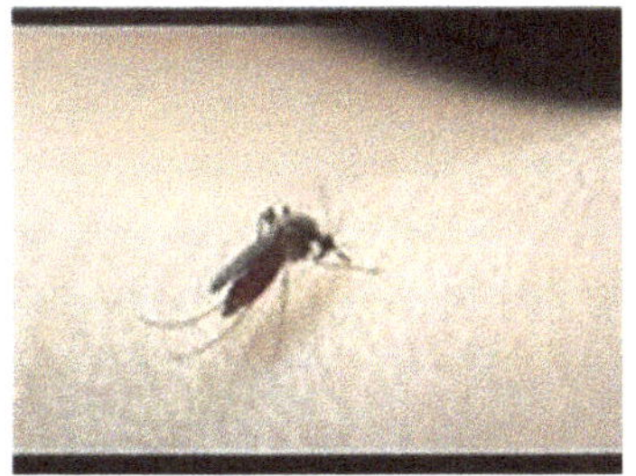 

A secondary coastal perimeter recon showed a secondary canal that entered into a small cave that went through Egypt to the Jordan inlet. They were very well hidden by the over curve made from surge waters and erosion over time. These might be reconned by some of the team or by the midget systems. This could have some strategic significance, even to the active NATO forces operating in the area of operations. It looked like a small canal that linked the Persian Gulf waters just to the other side of the Arabian Peninsula just West of Aden. All of this information could be used for contingency operations that almost always happen. Is there a possible extraction points for the prisoner's that had been located?

After six months of training like they were young guys again, but feeling the pain like we were seven hundred years old, they all decided after a good Cuban cigar and a few cocktails—old joints and some arthritis pain. They were well worth this task placed upon them. Sure, they felt the burden as Jesus Christ, our Holy Lord, saved us! It would all be worth the risk and, even more, seeing the reward of victory!

We all have the inner feeling like we are supposed to do something more or serve in some capacity. All of these brave men and contributors feel this same way! "May God be with us?"

The team is ready, and the next day we will begin the surveillance phase and leave back booby trap devices or "stay behinds" just in case there is an interested party on one or more of our systems inside of the enemies' base camp and area of operations.

Tomorrow T-Bone, Joey, and B. B. will deploy the ISR assets to allow the geologist and scientist to begin his plotting for detonation and full effect. The heavy movers will be used to carry in and stage the explosive chain. Entry points have been identified, but will need further recons completed from the smaller ISR assets.

During the team muster, all of the new information and intel had been identified. As a big plume of nice-smelling Cohiba cigar smoke glided past the screen, they all realized that they could actually get started and create the natural disaster. But no, there is always the intelligence-gathering part of every mission, with R&S that has to be completed. They had located so many hidden treasures, there must be more. A friendly SOF or SEAL team must be operating in this area. Before we initiated the disaster, we would check the area to be sure that no friendly forces were operating there.

It's no wonder why they had been denied to strike just when we had a key target in sight. There was some kind of connection, either investments or something that would further their cause or help in making someone wealthy or popular somehow. As our national strength was weakened, these extremist terrorists continued to mass and test their resolve on the world sanctions or threats. The only thing that these people understand is brutality! Let's bring it on then. Burn our 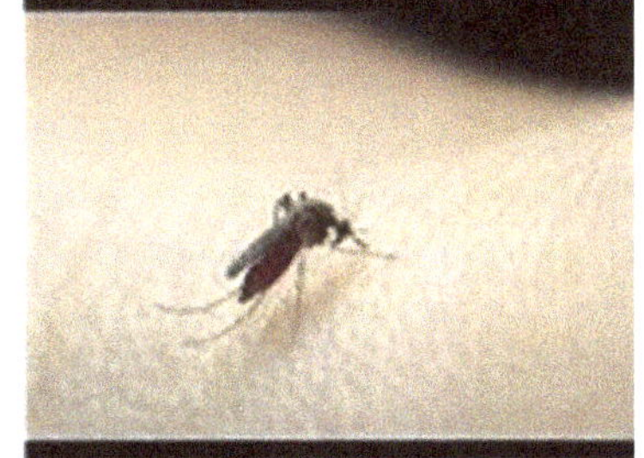 flag and chant your monkey language to Allah. You are gone!

For the team, the memories and experiences of seeing their buddies get blown up or die in their arms from an improvised explosive device (IED) or a stray bullet—that is what keeps these guys driven. It's having the gut instinct that something is wrong here and we will have to return to find the answers later. All of them are close to their retirement date or past it. All had planned to get out if they were ordered to return to their home base without cleaning up the mess or stomping terrorism so hard that it would be afraid to raise its ugly head anytime soon. And then there was another attack on a children's school with a VBIED (Vehicle-Borne Improvised Explosive Device) in a truck bomb filled with explosives. There were fifty dead from the school, including five teachers! The adrenalin pumped through every member of this team's veins and probably many other true patriots of America and the allies. The terrorists were planning on attacking the most treasured and valued assets of our nations, our children. There had been at least one strike on a school per week now. Each friendly nation had been hit by a terrorist attack since the inception of jihad, with the World Trade Center bombing, (9/11/2001). And our leadership still believed that this was only a crazed lone shooter, plus completely denied to say terrorism or A.Q.? Come on, wake up already! He has probably been paid a nice sum that is hidden somewhere. Ft. Hood, yeh. That was obvious that it was a lone gunman, along with some school shootings. Domestic violence has escalated. Either due to terrorist recruitment of weak and unpopular citizen's or mental illness that has been left unchecked for too long of a time? This must be identified and dealt with by properly trained medical and therapeutic professions.

Joey was one of our electronic technicians and an operator of our line of mini-might's, miniature vehicles for surveillance and sensor use, deployed in the late evening to early morning darkness. The transport UAV flew this tiny but mighty squadron of drone operators into action and slowed down enough for an easy drop onto some soft ground. "Game on!" Joey was hard at work and had deployed an ant unit to recon the Islamic National Highway closer to the borders of Iraq and Iran. They were receiving some radiological feedback from the sensors. They had the capability to send the trace codes for elements detected in the air.

From what the database was returning, it was nuclear radiation! Could they be close to the hidden and secret nuclear facility that the Islamic extremists have been ignoring the world's call to stop? The team had identified and located our base station for mission planning and operations command & control (C2). There would be two areas of employing the ISR assets and the big mother-load when ready. They would initiate from the northern area of the mountains bordering two enemy regions into the tunnels, and then with eyes on, it would be like a walk in the park!

They decided to try one of the mosquitoes with a tiny anthrax injection. It was close to a known test area for old Saddam and his WMD. There was a terrorist-looking soldier, nonmilitary but with a weapon outfit on. So the insect buzzed to his left shoulder and injected the piece of dirt. It only took thirty seconds, and this Tango was on the ground spewing some white-foaming snot- looking material from his mouth, and then died. Wow. We knew that this worked! Many of the guys watched in shock at the effect that they had just witnessed. Shit-Bag and Tony watched while smoking a nice Cohiba and drinking some fantastic Jeffeweissen Beer, which is only brewed in Belgium/Germany. Lucky for us, Predator had provided a pallet of cases of this nectar! A few more tests runs of our mini ISR drones would allow us to see if anything else was necessary before deploying the drone insect squadron into the area of operations.

There was one small ant patrol that followed into a deeper crack that took them into what could possibly be a geological and historical finding. It appeared to be a small religious room. It looked like a small Christian cathedral from ancient days. We could see a golden crucifix and some Trinity-stained glass images. This could be enormous, but the operation at hand had higher priority and was closer to Armageddon than anyone could believe!

There were many ancient carvings and scriptures in an old Hebrew language. We would record and maintain a copy of this if it could ever be revealed as a survey from some earlier times prior to the war. Otherwise, this place was ancient history, just as the rest of the area. Maybe it would just be buried again and geologists could return in a hundred years or so to research the area. They would just have to remember that CBRN materials had been involved in the region.

Joey moved a few of the ant drones closer to see if they could see or get some more positive information on this. This was the main target objective, after all! A. J. and B. B. watched to learn more about this system.

The lead recon ant moved through a tight crack in the tunnel rock wall. It began to show a vision of what seemed to be some kind of a laboratory setup. The ant provided the grid coordinates at 380 feet below the surface ground. That was all solid bedrock!

Suddenly Joey's excitement turned to frustration as the lead ant sensor recon unit went off and out of contact. It must have gotten too close to the radiation and melted, or perhaps something destroyed it. But the other ants that were just behind that one showed that the lead ant just stopped functioning. The best news of the day was what that tiny piece of technology could provide to this team—their target location and enough information to get started on the planning for this operation.

The intense excitement from what they had just witnessed was so exhilarating that it got everyone tired. So they decided to call it a day, and have a little celebration and decompression time as the end of a very successful day.

For security and fail-safe reasons, the team had split into two groups in two different geographical regions to prevent any compromise to or failure of this mission. It was much too important to only work from one site. Somewhere in the green rolling grasslands in the United Kingdom and the rolling mountains of Italy, there were some old underground bunker control areas of old military intelligence and weapons bases. These had all been refabricated and fitted to code with secure wiring to anti heat signature vents to everything that could be thought of. This way, they were invisible to the world! If the extremists' brotherhood had some kind of frequency secure zones that could be turned on and off at certain times of movement, the team could still function without interruption from two different sites and angles of penetration. They both had the same perks: fitness training center, indoor shooting range, kitchen chef, and so on. Whenever they had to move some equipment, conduct training, or move supplies, then they would turn on their own security bubble that blocked communication signals, views, and everything that was not to be seen. When in the operational bunker, all countersecurity measures went into effect.

From the extremist violations to the global authorities' sanctions and Peace Accords on creating WMD, they were sure to be in the toilet now. Captain Morgan, Steve and Pete, the team commanders, wrote the After-Action Report (AAR) and sent it to our secret connection within the Networked Security Alliance and passed on that the mission was now officially a go!

Morgan and Clutch sat back with good cigars and a cool cube-libre. The day was good! Clutch was available to the team for mechanical and engineering support on a part time basis. An old and trusted friend of the captain, Predator had worked out these contacts to be able to be brought in secretly as needed.

Note: Predator is part of team Jaguar as the 'Coordinator and narrator for this story'.

Line drawn in to show the geological fault line (Caliphahtta Shiitemzehlffah Fault).

With this fault crossing the many branches from the INH, there will be thousands of hidden tunnels, caches of weapons, and even some important unknown artifacts that could be a great find for scientists. This is said to be a very strong and dangerous fault line that could trigger some of the worst earthquakes ever seen in history. It is a very large and fractured tectonic plate that has been broken many times, as can be seen by the jagged edges and shape. The last earthquake in this region was less than one year ago. The team has felt some small tremors at times. Area #1 is located closer to the target area, while Area #2 is located close by in a west Europe NATO nation. The complexes are duplicates of each other; each has all the necessary high-technology systems and capabilities. The team functions like one that is together. Although the team is split between two physical site areas, they all communicate and work together in a virtual manner daily. Wiki, research.

The INH crosses cutoff tunnels that head in opposite directions, to cover the Arab nations' most important areas of operation for trade or war.

The majority of the INH runs the full length of the fault line and has branches that cross it in many places; almost every hundred meters, a tunnel branches off. This will make the placement and positioning of the explosive, the powder keg, function significantly well. The tunnels will get most of the overpressure, and CBRN elements will be released into the air as well! We will benefit from the fine element of surprise. When can an insect not be trusted? We are forever evolving as our enemies continue to try and destroy us. With so many new and improved devices, they will not know what hit them when it does so.

From the explosive train staged along the INH will be completely annihilated from the overpressure and CBRN elements that are blown through the tunnels. The shock wave will collapse the underground network with a few heavier grade explosives strategically placed to expand the destructive range of this "natural disaster".

Be proud and support our brave armed forces that protect everyone's God-given rights and freedoms. Be ever so vigilant because this nation has been compromised by unsecured borders and weakness in leadership!

Chapter Two
Who Controls the Media?

The news is filled with topics like political corruption, disasters, death, same-sex relationships, and so on. It's awful! It certainly is not what our scriptures tell us to do or be like. Many need to read the Holy Bible more in order to better understand what is expected from them; they should be trying to fulfill these requirements the best that they can. No one on this earth is perfect, but with strong faith and a relationship with our Lord Jesus Christ, we can overcome and see his potential for each of us.

The media has people controlled to believe almost any nonsense they publish, whether the truth is staring them in the face or not. Some media stations were forced and funded handsomely to smear deceptive media information. In the narcissistic psychotic minds of these extremist Jihadists desperate steps to gain control, these Extremists had no idea what was coming their way.

Once you begin to hear or read a news story, it can make you wonder if the media think that the masses are just stupid and blind. Or does the enemy own and control the stories? The liberal media only writes what will make the readers believe in this political administration, and no matter how bad this administration is doing and ruining this nation, the media is owned and supported by the liberal administration. Mis-information is sometimes used as a tool by corrupt states or agencies to try to gain the public majority to believe that they are the victims or have been wronged in some way by another.

There is a story in the paper about the allied nations, mostly America, bombing innocent civilians in Iraq and Afghanistan, but this story doesn't come close to the truth according to a special operations buddy who was on this so-called disaster of a mission. "The terrorists came up from a tunnel and selected a house to use as an ambush site for the NATO convoys that would pass by. They killed the family, and then when the NATO forces returned fire, it almost looked as if those forces had killed the family, as the terrorists slipped back underground and to a safe escape. The media is either called in ahead of time or a cameraman is staged to film the cover-up and place the blame on NATO. Mis- information in process". This negative propaganda is presented to the entire world. But is everyone blind? Wake up before it is too late and possibly becomes a reality.

The Islamic National Highway is a tunnel network that connects the Middle Eastern nations together and provides covert movement out of sight as they resupply targeted areas.

If the media can distort the truth so much as to convince people to believe their view over the truth, it could even be possible to infiltrate other nations' leadership and sway the public into believing that the media's man is a better choice than their own countryman. Some nations have already been compromised, and the public media played a tremendous role in power persuasion or brainwashing the desperate, needy, self-centered individuals to actually believe the load of manure that the candidate was promising to give to them. This chaos could be enormous! It could start another revolutionary war or even more. A present empire might implode before our very eyes.

It started some twelve years or so earlier from this one president's ideology and flat-out experience at conning people, combined with inept abilities as a leader and how to manage a free nation's issues. His inactions caused the security and the economy of the United States to snowball another ten years with the effects from the damage that had already been done to bring this nation to internal division and chaos, with the world financial districts feeling the damage also. Yes, he was "slick." What a traitorous bastard, though! All of the blood spilled from those sacrificing everything in the name of God and their country because of some self-righteous egotistic prick! A narcissistic wannabe that could not even find his own arse if it wasn't running all of the time.

It's as if we ran an ad: "President wanted. Qualifications: must have a high school degree or GED as a minimum. Accepting applications from neighborhood watch coordinators, janitors, etc. Leadership experience will help!" Maybe we should have placed an ad in the Classifieds Section: "HELP WANTED: Leader. Must possess leadership skills and have served in the military for a minimum of four years to apply. College degrees will help."

Think of the costs we have paid trying to preserve freedom, against the peaceniks and psychos who are trying to create problems on a global scale. In a free nation, the people have the right to vote and elect whom they think is best for the position. In some situations, the weaker of the candidates in the election is selected, and then is the new leader. In four years, he can show what he can do for the country. Some of it is good, some bad, and some disagreed upon. However, this is what the majority elected, so the people have to deal with it the best they can. When a problem arises, he is fueling an aircraft to fly him to some emergency meeting, fund raiser or vacation with the family.

Things have become so distorted from what is seen and heard that only certain supporting comrades can watch the news or skim through newspapers to see if anything is worth bringing to the attention of the team so as not to distract them from the mission. Mostly it's just more racial hatred and crime, more political controversy as usual.

Better just to remain focused on the mission than to be disturbed or angered by that garbage!

The global economy seems to have taken a downward spiral? Not sure if that is from bad accounting or the oil misers' fault. Just more to play into another natural disaster in this place. Of course, there would be an article prefabricated and fed to the various media agencies to give them a story. Then they could distort it and spice it up any way that they wanted. After all, all that matters to them is that maybe they will win a Pulitzer Prize for writing or get some promotion from the boss for their story.

And the Benghazi, U.S. Embassy attack cover-up is still being pushed into the shadows. "Disgraceful" from all points of view, but soon to be redeemed from the personnel from the Embassy area that will testify and tell the investigative team what really happened. This mixed with the Patriotic Pentagon staffer's will determine those at fault and their punishment!

A multi-ethnic black man, a Muslim, was elected as president of the United States. He even started the Democratic Convention with a Muslim prayer. This was never reported by the liberal media. That should have awakened some of those who were sleeping on their feet and just moving with the party that they thought was best to manage and lead a great nation. But they have no one. Not one citizen could believe what they were hearing. Now they knew, that this is a leaderless nation.

Now knowing for certain that the world had been compromised and it really was in God's hands and his control. So this might be what the Lord wanted them to do. They were all very strong in their faith with Christianity and Jesus Christ/ here had never been so much racial division in this nation's history.

The question, however, was still how and where did the security get breached and how many politicians and others might have known about this conspiracy to try and bring down America and other nations. Were they still around to be located, or did they luck out and die before they could be interrogated and castrated by an angry American patriot and veteran to the armed forces who dedicated twenty or more years of his life to that duty?

Politicians are applying laws and rules that dictate how a terrorist prisoner is interrogated. It should be as an enemy combatant, thank you. They can cut someone's head off and video it for the world to see. Yet these rules now state that the prisoner cannot be harmed or physically tortured during interrogations that could provide very important information for the good guys. No, do not hurt their feelings!

A terrorist does not fall under our national laws, only international law and the Geneva Convention. They do not follow these themselves. Duke said that he doesn't care about laws when it comes to this scum! They have killed enough of ours, probably equivalent to one of their nations.

That's fine; there are always other ways to get the job done. A peaceful, kinder, gentler conglomerate of nations will not be fighting this war that terrorism has picked with us. We did not go looking for a place to start a war—they did! Any other logic on this issue is naive and pure ignorance. We will use different tactics altogether and win this fight for our brothers and for our nation and our children's futures!

Before impeachment proceedings begin, he will have either started a religious war or racial war?

Sometime in December 2012, there were two earthquakes that hit Iran. They were around the 6.5 to 7.0 magnitude on the seismograph chart machine. What was this? The news spread like wildfire around the world. The test was complete. The team tested one charge, and the other was a real quake, in different locations along the fault line. This was to see if the plan could work as designed. The ignition charge will be the five-hundred-pound underwater Shape-Charge Nuke to set the fault into activity. Whether it causes the earthquake is unknown, but this will be what the geological center (NOAA) picks up on their machines as the epicenter. This can be tactically set in place by a variety of ways—dropped from a variety of air or water assets. The team / Predator had said that " can select these assets of willing drivers when the cash negotiation is completed. The method of deployment will not be known. All that the carrier will know is that it is a man-made scientific system device to help grow coral reefs and protect coastlines from natural storms and water surge/erosion"?

Chapter Three
Cause and Effect

Let me introduce Jack, nicknamed Captain Morgan. He's a SEAL who retired in 2006, with a wife and two grown children in their thirties; he has four grandkids.

Jack is noted for his love of rum. The counterespionage intelligence specialist also loves to feed counter stories to various media reporters about any issues that indicate that they may have been compromised or that the real news is not getting reported and that vindicate the allied nations from any misleading stories about military operations in or near the same area of operations where the team is working.

Some of the equipment and support technicians stay in the barn/bunker and relay information to the team during training about possible overflying aircraft that might be part of the enemy's surveillance information-gathering assets to see who is doing what and where. They definitely need to take these precautionary measures learned from field experience and the Persian Gulf War. There have already been enough special operations recon team sightings in all of the Arab nations of cave holes where they got in and out of the underground network in the past week.

It was almost time to begin plotting and marking out the route to start from and all the key target areas in the geo-spatial plane to trigger the effects needed and intended to be successful. All of the research would be placed into a LIDAR map that only appears when a flashlight is focused on the blank map material (almost like a flexible plastic). The images, terrain, and marked targets or buildings all appear in a 3D-type of image raised straight up from the map.

Using the large plotting table with the imaging systems that show the terrain and scale really brings the entire area to life. It makes you feel like a giant looking down on the earth. When the techs draw in the points and special areas of interest, it really makes you feel like you are right there. George recommended that they do a trial run with the 4x4 all-terrain flatbed vehicle with one hundred pounds tied to the cargo bed.

This is to simulate the movement of the systems and to make sure that an explosive booby trap does not destroy one of these extremely powerful and expensive systems. It's better to run a practice test prior to assembling the entire fault field line. This will permit the team to prepare and stage all of the systems so that they will all function as designed. We want to simulate an actual earthquake, and that is what it will be.

Since Israel is the target in this region that we need to support, the patrol will begin from Israel and stretch through all of the surrounding nations. Crossing the Gulf or any rivers will not be a problem as long as the percussion can be projected to the next sensor in the explosives chain to connect all Islam territories on the African Cape Horn. Many tunnels and subterranean canals show that they connect Egypt and Yemen and any of the other Muslim friends would be destroyed from this disaster. If they cannot be reached due to connecting tunnels along the fault line, then they will be hit with armies of toxic insects to spread the nerve agents throughout the region. The bats could fly into the intercontinental canal and drop CBR pellets that would burst open and make the entire canal and pathways toxic to anything that breathes air to survive. We need to cover all bases and threat areas. "Stated Predator". Should this actually trigger a real earthquake then this could be the true ending of a Barbaric Empire. Maybe destiny awaits and the team is the trigger point?

From the many missed meetings and conferences with the western leader and most powerful ally, there were mixed feelings and ideas of how much this leader would support and aid in the protection from the Arab region that surrounds Israel, this small Christian homeland.

The Muslim and Islamic religious fanatics are enemies to the small Jewish nation of Israel.

A simple line cannot be drawn to tell these Muslim terrorists that they must not cross beyond this point or there will be retaliation. They do not care about any of this. They cause disturbances to keep the press and media on a certain topic, anything other than any construction of nuclear weapons or the western leader being a Muslim himself. This compromises the supreme military in the world and this nation that was the shining beacon in the distance that represented freedom. Enemies do face consequences.

Time was beginning to run out, and they would need to elevate the timeline and movement into the area of operations. The time fuse was the clock. And it was ticking.

The geologist and some other specialists have completed some calculations and points on the map for the placement of the detonation to cause the desired effect and cave in like a huge sinkhole into the earth. UAV Drones will fly the heavy load vehicles to the perspective entry points for them to deliver their explosive payloads to the strategic point in the INH as planned for. The parachutes will have a quick release when the vehicle and cargo have touched down onto the ground. Then these special designed parachutes will disintegrate to ashes and there is no trace of enemy or foreign intrusion to the territory.

The reconnaissance and surveillance has been done of the matrix of underground tunnels created over the centuries from water erosion and slaves and prisoners used to dig, widen, and reinforce the walls and overhead to be like a bunker from land bombings, explosives, or any kind of penetration. This is the main reason why the team lead and scientists thought that it would be best to map the entire underground highway system prior to moving in further.

They planned on utilizing all of the arsenal or supply models of sensor drones to achieve this for them. They would sit in their planning room with the conferencing screen. This way, as the intelligence and engineers moved and drove these systems down into the underground complex, the entire team could have real-time eyes on the target. The engineers did a fantastic job of sketching the overlay of how this underground network would look if simulated or raised aboveground. This would also provide the entire team with knowledge of the plan. They could easily switch job positions, if need be, while the operational movement and placement of the explosives and safety stay-behinds, or booby traps, were being set into place. Any enemy that might slip upon something would be taken out of the picture before even realizing that he had just discovered something strange. Every detail was being well thought out and tested by simulation techniques. Some sensors showed imagery of a pile of human skeletons that was like a dump site to hide these people that had been killed or died in some way that they were hastily dumped in a tunnel entrance?

The next day, was going to be a fun and interesting day. A little distraction and entertainment combined with exercise, of course. Each site would rotate the following day so that everyone on the team had this experience and workout.

The team had some common friends and set up a small medieval village mock-up. They/ the team, were going to have a day like maybe a few generations back might have lived. There would be a horseback attack on an enemy village and staging area. The weapons were all swords, axes, and so on. The targets would be fake straw men with mixed fruit parts blended in for effect—like a melon as the head. There would be some obstacle courses built into the scenario, like rope climbs, swings, moats to jump just wide enough for these horses to be able to make. Training the riders to command and befriend the animals to listen could take some time. So once a week, they would all go out and ride their new friends and teammates, so to speak. It was some fun training and preparation mixed together. These horses would be an escape plan for them if somehow compromised? As thorough as this plan has been prepared and the high level of sensor technology would make it close to if not impossible. Maybe at the very end the team may ride their friends to the departure platform before having them returned to the kind new friend and farmer that had lent them to the team. If anything, this training and exercise was to bring out the primal warrior instincts in man and to have fun while playing the mockup setting. Each site would conduct this scenario so the other could manage all of the sensor devices control and monitoring systems so there were no delays with their mission. A seamless operation.

The next day after the teams new experience and sore butts from riding horses so rigorously, a good Jacuzzi soak and rest was needed before continuing the mission plan. The site managers switched to allow the entire team to experience this activity.

They would need to determine each nation's threat level and proximity to prepare the induced fault line to create the payback for all of the innocent lives lost from terrorism attacks, including "accidents" caused by evil participation to make them occur, such as an unexplainable train derailment or in-flight airliner explosion. There was a plan to drop leaflets in all civilian regions to notify them of an impending natural disaster that was coming. The leaflets would explain to them that their government does not care, and that they should not consider it as a ticket to martyrdom, but rather as a call to move to the farthest-away coast, whether north or south. The team was still working on the best way to deliver this message and not leave any evidence behind. There were many ideas of the disappearing ink on disintegrating paper, etc.

Another R&S fly had been sitting on a wall in a cavern-like conference room. There were some high-ranking Extremist leaders there from splinter error cells. The team's Arabic translators and techs sat around the monitor trying to decipher the entire conversation and orders being given by one of the older-looking jihadists. They understood, Sleeper cells sent into all nations decades in the past to create a global financial meltdown from within! "By undermining the GDP of each nation, and placing them in deep debt!" Intel Tommy said, "This sounds like a global conspiracy to take over with jihad." Predator replied that "He had had a conversation with another female shadow agent that assisted his missions; prior to secretly plan the constructing of this special team Jaguar". "He had listened to her explain about a terrorist theory that her agents and special teams were able to interrogate and collect some important software full of tactical plans, places and dates. Some names were already deceased from acting against our NATO Forces".

The team remembered the secretive political conspiracies that surrounded the Americans and the compromise of secret intelligence; and how a new president was the first multiethnic Arab Balsharack Inowhanna. This junior senator had little experience but was trained to give speeches well by the use of a tele-prompter. His memory is just as weak as his spine, "said Duke" How can any of us have been so overshadowed? Evil is what this jihad is, just like the Crusade in the Christian days thousands of years ago. Jihad is pure evil by nature and can destroy humanity as we know it. The team drafted a letter, encrypted, to Predator, as "Highly T. S. / meaning of high importance and in military terms "Top Secret". This brings all of the pieces of the puzzle together now!" I often used to think of how this could be happening. The head terrorist, now dead, had planned and learned well. He studied our legal and financial systems and everything else to understand our vulnerability. Very clever, and now let's hope that we can get this to the intelligence networks that can do something about it!

Predator will know who to pass this to and will make certain that our allies understand also. That way no one person can be compromised and prevented from sharing this news with the correct high-level agencies that can bring justice to those involved in this global conspiracy. We know that it has already begun, because there are nations in financial turmoil and chaos. With each nation's compromised "Department of Injustice", the train wreck is already in motion. Now to stop and prevent this?

The Americans will bring swift justice by investigations, imprisonment with impeachment, or a heavier sentence than he, "the leaderless wonder" would have seen if back in his homeland—more like a lynching.

The team reflected on having targets of opportunity in their sights, and then Washington refusing to let them take them out. This caused much anger, frustration, and disgust within the operator realm. "Now this all makes sense," Morgan had said.

The terrorists worked to get their own people into the highest positions in government and military, becoming the very fabric of our society. Then they attacked our embassies and murdered an ambassador to this raghead nation. The guards were murdered, and the facility ransacked; they crossed our line! 1, 2, 3, that was it. It would take a secretive group of trained strategists to unravel this mess. There must first be a general reduction of government agencies and a house cleaning to take out the lame, trash that is old and just sitting around. Replace the ignorant and older minded ones just hanging onto their positions and bring in some fresh intelligent thinkers and problem solvers to the White House. This will be a good place to start in the restructuring and adjusting of government agencies that work for the people of the nation. The Captain was just decompressing some from some of the chaos and shady actions that had been used recently "to cover one's ass", so to speak. Pete stated, "I believe that we all have a responsibility in life and a destiny, I believe that we have reached our moment". Now justice can prevail, and our citizens can get on with their lives that God had planned for. He never said that it would be a cakewalk and that we would not face challenges. We just need to see what the challenge is and not ignore anything evil. That is why we were given intelligence to think on our own and follow God's word in the Holy Bible, where he left scriptures that others wrote about him. Thank you for allowing us this opportunity to prevent this evil plan!

Predator took the message and had it encrypted to three trustworthy old friends in national intelligence positions in various friendly nations. This would better prepare them for the ransacking of this plan.

Jihad is the Arabic word meaning Holy War. Just like the Christian Crusades many centuries ago. This is not a game or something made up for fun; these people have declared war on Christians and want to kill all of us. Understand this, and you and yours might survive. Do nothing, and suffer the consequences. The Middle East is still happy to live like they are still in the 1600s or earlier. With high ambitions to achieve obtaining nuclear weapons, these fanatics must be stopped at any cost. They live under strict religious and barbaric oppression. No civilized government is going to change a culture that has lived like that for so many centuries.

The one thing that was still in question was the financing and where it was coming from. Some investments and company transactions are shady, and trillions of dollars can disappear from where they were intended to go. Many of these issues came about just when a man with an Arabic name who also had US citizenship became known as an inexperienced senator who was going to try to run for president of the United States. There were many skeptics and questions raised about his patronage, qualifications, and so on. Yet he was pushed through. Many screamed about a corrupt system. After all, his opponent was a combat war hero, with years of political experience and leadership.

As Captain Morgan said, "If you think that everything is peaceful and calm, just because you have that privilege where you might live, you need to open your eyes and mind and research the world and see how other cultures live and what their laws are like." If you are young enough and want to contribute in helping your country, join the military and travel the world. Get the education, knowledge, and benefits that you could not get by just going to college. A man could learn honor, integrity, character, and responsibilities and have a true sense of patriotism to his country, all while earning a paycheck each month on top of everything else. The military offers so many options for someone to actually work in a career field that he or she likes and better prepare him or herself for the future. Most young people are just misguided by what they hear from people who are afraid and would not fight if death were staring them in the face. Run and hide in Canada or somewhere? Will that make you feel proud to tell people later in life that you were afraid so you ran to hide? Doesn't that make you feel proud? You at least need to understand your country's heritage and do your part in improving or keeping it safe!

Do not be a coward. Be productive and make your country proud! Research your candidate before just voting. Select the best person for the job, by experience, knowledge, and so on. Skin color should not have any weight on any voters' decision. Just the best and most experienced person for this highest position in government.

Fill your heart and soul with pride. The military will not just make you a better person; you will learn more, understand life better, and be a stronger individual. We are in a war, with a new type of warfare; now called asymmetric warfare. It is not like any of the traditional methodology; it is more equivalent to western styles of smaller militia or special operations teams that can strike and be on the move. The line between good and evil is blurred because the enemy blends into the population or region to strike anytime and anywhere. The enemy will use any weapon that can cause the most destruction and chaos, with no thought of consequences. In the U.S. the Internal Revenue Service was caught in a controversial political scandal. However, there will always be consequences to hostile actions/ scandals to weaken or disrupt the function of any large department or government agency?

Each generation has the responsibility to instill strong cultural values and virtues into the newer generations in order to preserve a nation's strength and patriotism to their heritage. Otherwise, the people become weak and expect that the present privileges will stay as the present free state. Each empire has fallen due to this lethargy and false senses of security and truth of the situation. Government subsidization began to be manipulated by the poverty-level, unmotivated people who did not care about finding a job to contribute to making the nation stronger, and that leads to debt and the taxpayers having to take care of the mindless people who would rather just get whatever the system would give to them as long as it is free! With the Civil Rights Act of the 1960s, the organization called the NAACP oversees that black people are not being forgotten about, but rather receive special attention within society. This was mainly a group of so-called religious leaders who were trying to find some fame or have a legacy that they did something good. All that I have ever seen is the stirring up of racial hatred, all driven from slavery and Civil War days. Hypocrisy at its best. There should not be any racial tensions since the "Civil Rights Movement", was approved and made law. Follow Dr. M.L.K. and learn from him, not these disgraced stands in speaker's that do not speak the words of Dr. King!

It is history that they cannot leave alone; they do not have complete understanding of how and why there were slaves brought over on cargo vessels across the ocean from Africa. African traders themselves sold their prisoners, the mentally ill, and whomever they thought that they could sell to this new land. There was a great need for farm workers to pick crops for selling in this land, as well as for trade with other countries. They were essentially given meals, shelter, and wages for helping the landowner. Then they started to be called slaves, because they were sold to the crop owners. By providing your child with a good education, they will be more capable of understanding and at making clear decisions on their own. Ignorance will just cause divisiveness and bad decisions for important issues. Ignorance and complacency will get you nowhere in life or to become a productive citizen.

After a certain length of time, a white president wanted to create into law the abolishment of slavery. Meaning that no man can own any other human being, for any reason. This was fought over by the northern and southern states' armies during the Civil War, and the slaves were released; some were even given parcels of land and provisions to create a normal life for their families. There was much division between the founding Caucasians and the black people, who had not been correctly introduced; it was not correctly explained who they were and where they had come from. To the Caucasian majority and others, the Africans seemed alien. Nowadays the black community is the majority or they appear to be, and a minority of them are intelligent intellectuals who do not stand for handouts or complete rule from any government. The entire handout generation of mixed ethnic groups started much division within the nation between the wage earners who paid their taxes and the federal government welfare and handout mind-set of certain people; these latter wanted to take the easy road instead of living an honest day's pay and fulfilling what society is supposed to do. They are making the mightiest nation in the world weak and shameful. History is being written that everyone, no matter the ethnic group, who is not working but is living from government handouts, does not help the overall economic function of a free nation. When people work and provide for their families, some of the taxes paid go to maintain the infrastructure and public utilities systems. There has been a complete bluff pulled on these individuals who would cave from standing for freedom and our constitutional laws, which have been trampled upon by this unknown Marab, multiethnic Arab. Investigations are dividing this nation more today because of the nigorants/ ignorance of all races or ethnic groups that follow the lead of this abomination! Although the majority of African American's might be a small percentage in comparison to other ethnic groups the vast majority of African American's due live off of federal hand-outs as percentages of other ethnic groups also choose to do. This is not good for any nation's economy, and only emboldens the government to expand and eventually take total control in the form of Socialism, Fascism, and Dictatorship. "It also gives the perception of ignorance and weakness to other tax paying citizens that are forced to pay for this federal aid to the lame or lazy citizen's that believe that they are doing what is easiest for themselves. This does not gain respect from any of the majority taxpayers. "You will not be respected unless it is obvious that you are disabled and cannot work. Otherwise, you need to get a job"!

Chapter Four
Lessons Learned? Or the Past Repeating Itself?

Everything is driven by money, greed, and power. Energy is a big cover scheme to bring in investors with lots of money to keep the programs going and those involved quite comfortable. Meanwhile, the hardworking, God-fearing taxpayer lives with an unknown burden that is wasting their money and investments for a better future.

There was always someone, somewhere in a news article or television show saying that this is wrong and that someone needs to do something about this.

The usual answer from some cronies would be to write your legislators or governor. That fell on deaf ears.

That's another reason why this group got back together. Not everyone can just sit back and say, "Nothing can be done; just live with it." Government scandals, coverups and conspiracies. The IRS scandal, Embassy attacks, etc.!

The Jihadists are increasing the threat that they are acquiring nuclear material. They, of course, said that the nuclear reactors were for energy and peaceful means only—not to produce weapons. But "If it smells and looks like something, then it is!" And certainly, the terrorist nations are plotting more attacks. It was all discovered—and was very amusing to the team—that they had the facility underground, inside of a mountain. They were just above the general area of where the fault line split and went in different directions that would take out the majority of the Arab world's continent should there be a massive earthquake. With the proper placement of high explosives, all problems can be solved. A chain reaction of highly sensitive, acoustically detonated tactical nukes along the proposed fault line would project something similar. The majority of information collected from terrorists has been helpful in guiding this team as well as other active-duty military units to various caches or training areas.

Israel might feel some tremors or have some tidal surge on its shoreline. But Israel would have no worries about having to take out or start a nuclear war.

NATO nations have finally realized the magnitude of the global situation and terror infiltration. New identification methods have begun to be used to protect the most classified information, infrastructures, and safe havens.

The terrorist nations and extremists have lived a life of brutality and tribal clans against one another for generations, trying to wipe out other clans or regions for the land. They have killed their own in cold blood for not following the extremists' views or laws. Many have been hidden away in underground prisons, where they have no idea if they will ever see daylight again. Some of these cached prisons have been located in Afghanistan and Pakistan in recent years. Some of the citizens and soldiers found there have said that they had been there for years. All of them were very skinny and sick from malnourishment and mistreatment. This is like the barbarian days, and the past is beginning to come unraveled on these dictators and these religions. Two American Journalists are reported to be in these prisons. (Received from friendly intelligence/HUMINT).

New technologies for R&S and C4I began to be implemented and tested. Some were even placed in drone satellites carried by test rockets into space.

This CT System/ Counterterrorism would sense if any countermeasures were being used by the enemy, and then at various times send pulses into mountain ranges or any suspected subterranean hideouts, caches, and so on. This would provide rapid information to response teams or systems. A new style of warfighting with technologies has begun to be noticed as a reality to modern day threats and adversary surveillance or strikes?

This FU-II device provided the team with actionable intelligence as to where the targets lay. They were too deep for a man to get to, so the M&M unit would need to be used. The miniaturized mechanized units would get through the cracks and crevices in the earth to reach them for the team, these miniaturized vehicles, like remote-controlled Tonka trucks, could carry a surveillance package made to fit the landscape or drop off a miniature bomb, just as evolution in technologies and research has made our scientists smarter, we have created similar effects from lesser amounts for the desired outcome.

It just so happens, that defense satellites picked up radiation hot spots close to the main Islam extremist terrorist nation, which has lied about their nuclear weapons containment facility. The satellites also showed proof that there had been a practice nuclear detonation test close to the underground facility. Similar siting's in the Asian nations that have not been compliant have also been identified. This has provided the team with some more valuable information. The INH runs within 500 meters from this very site. Could the extremists be planning on moving a weapon closer to their target? This is going to hasten the mission even more now that there is proof of the international nuclear sanctions being defied and the fact that these extremists have just kept on moving with the construction of their facility as well as their ultimate plan to destroy Christianity all over the world.

With this underworld of tunnel systems and highways, the Islamic community has been able to move and hide many things that we have not known about throughout history. The possibilities of what might be found could be endless: weapons or financial caches of kings or princes. Soon everything will be known, at least to a point. The sensors will locate larger entry points to bring in the weight-carrying, remote-controlled vehicles. Then the explosive train can be set. The only thing remaining is the time left on the fuse. They will be delivered by remote pilot of a UAV helicopter or drone to carry the payload and deliver it to the nearest entry point to stage in the chain.

Initially, there was a point discovered where caves met the waterline of the Caspian Sea, as well as the Gulf of Oman and the Persian Gulf also. The cave was an entry and escape route from the tunnels as a last chance in the case of compromise and total destruction. Two of our younger members, who are in better condition, are Tony and Chuck. Chuck has a prosthetic right leg from a roadside IED that blew up the Humvee that he was riding in as machine-gunner during Operation Desert Storm. He was one of the first of our wounded while hunting this terrorist scum.

Both Tony and Chuck are avid kayakers and could easily swoop into there at night, being undetected because of the small signature and sleek design of the kayak. If there were any wave swells that would roll the kayak and not just pass over smoothly, these guys would do what is called a barrel roll and commit a 360-degree roll and return straight up again. They would do a quick recon and deploy a few sensors and stay behind explosive booby trap devices to catch anyone that may have caught them on any surveillance devices of their own. We know that the terrorists receive armament and technology from some Communist and other terror nations. So, we must plan accordingly.

Tony and Chuck would have a bag full of drone bats, which could fly by radar and sonar just like a real bat. These special bats were to be utilized for the mapping and location of certain missed tunnels. They could seek and identify, while providing the team with the full-screen visual R&S data needed. Their location beacons would emit a short pulse every few seconds to sketch the path and pass the sub-geographic locations.

We can send in M&M Team 1, with the flies, ants, and spiders. We may as well send in some mosquitoes carrying the plague, anthrax, and malaria to infect some of the underground workers and hopefully put some fear into the remaining staff about working there, thus slowing down their evil plan, while providing data to the World Saviors Team, as they had been dubbed earlier by friends in the Inner circle of this team.

Once these vehicles penetrated through some small cracks or holes, they would soon lead right into one of the main tunnel routes. Here they would drop small, pebble-like sensors that were colored to match the earth-toned colors of the region. No one would ever notice or have any idea that these sensors were set and feeding all kinds of data for the scientists to study air quality, sound, movement, and so on.

The entire world did not know that some of the events and actions were planned to make it look like America was falling apart and the military was ordered to leave the region. Even the American people were up in arms and could not understand why such an inexperienced, Muslim-named junior politician had been ejaculated into office. The entire scenario and economic collapse was a planned farce, to make the terrorists think that we were giving up and leaving. There was another actual plan in place to strike the nuclear site as soon as they became cocky enough to threaten someone with their nuclear weapons. First, they would have to conduct test fires of certain missiles that could carry the weapon. That would put the world on advanced alert that there would be a portion of the Arab world disappearing shortly. And better than this, no one who was not supposed to, knew about the team's mission. The geologist and scientists helping already had a press release ready and all of the answers to how the earth sometimes has these earthquakes as the internal magma moves the plates about. When there is a collision along a fault line, this normally causes an effect similar to a train wreck.

Instead of a missile with a warhead, we can use a remote drone snake that can get to the location and detonate as if a tactical weapon had been set off.

Insects from common areas can be manufactured to function as miniature surveillance cameras—just like the saying, "What I would give to be a fly on the wall." We can listen and see everything, like being in the same room. With technology like this available, the injured team members who can barely walk from combat and training injuries can now sit at computer console desks and operate remote and virtually.

One more week of training before the team conducts their first trial run.

Most of the new C4ISR technologies will be used, and if necessary, the fireworks also. (Command, Control, Computers, Communications) Intel/Surveillance, Recon.

They are hoping for a quiet trial run. There is always the chance that something could happen. Compromise is not an option with this plan, so no prisoners and no witnesses will be able to spread any advance warning of the intentions to come in the very near future.

The reconnaissance drones would also have the capability to drop small amounts of CBR, nerve agents. This would also avoid compromise because they would only cause seizure-like activity and not be lethal; the result of an attack would appear more as a medical condition than anything else. Plus there have been so many chemical, biological, radiological (CBR) materials moved through these tunnels, that the terrorists might well think they caused it from error. Some prior and present terror leaders have hidden their arsenals of CBR agents and gasses in underground caches. This is known, even though proof has only been found in Iraq. It was one reason why we could not get commanders' approval to go into tunnel entries or caves—which still remains a standing order to operators in the A.O.

From this initial trial run of the M&M ant brigade, they have shown us where some caches of some explosives and nerve agents have been hidden. We will need to get them in closer to decipher the warning labels that are placed on the containers. They are written in Arabic, Chinese, and what appears to be Russian. They seem to look very aged from the monitor. This could also mean that they are extremely unstable. The ants do not pick up any security, so we are certain that there must be some explosive booby traps farther down each side of the tunnel to prevent anyone not allowed from getting to them. This will be a perfect drop-off point for one of our powder kegs. Just as planned, the nerve agents will keep scientists and reporters away from the area. The Investigators will assume that the preplanned earthquake must have ruptured these military/terrorist caches and restrict the area and attempt to decontaminate as much of the

surrounding area as possible. After seeing the worker next to you melt inside of his deacon suit and then combust, everyone will stay clear!

Chapter Five
Flight Risks

After multiple attempted attacks that failed and a few by lone gunmen that were successful, most of Muslim origin from the Middle East, we often wondered what "intelligence" meant. How could these people have multiple citizenships in other countries and still be able to freely fly back and forth and no one suspected anything? The very people who are paid to keep an eye out for suspicious activity noticed nothing. But some of our rules spank the hand of anyone who stereotypes those of religious or ethnic persuasions.

Chuck, Robbie, Pete and a few others on the team were debating some security issues. Steve said, "To me, an Arab carrying two passports would raise a red flag immediately".

"Flying under the radar" is what it is called. It is also called "counter surveillance." There are still some areas that need to be tightened up, but much of the new technology is very advanced for our day and age. Surveillance picks up a potential terrorist in an air terminal or train station. Suddenly a small fly lands on him and bites him, putting him into a seizure, because the mechanical fly or mosquitoes injected a toxin into him. Security reacts and places him onto a stretcher, acting like paramedics. They complete a full exam for the crime center to determine if he is on their list and who he is. Then, if they determine they have a terrorist, they can bring him into the

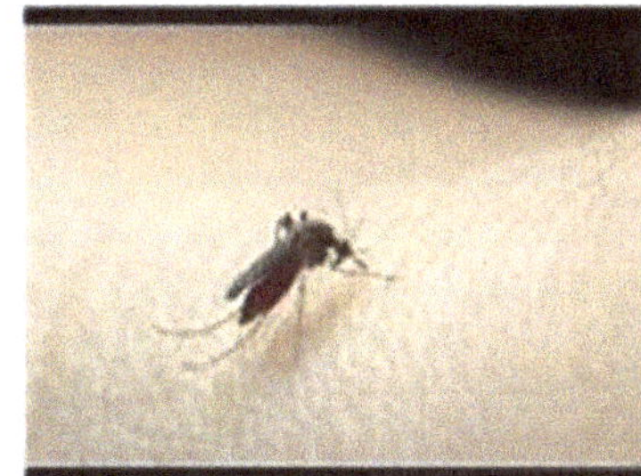

interrogation room. If not, they file his information for possible future use, and release him as if he just had some kind of reaction to something, telling him to take a few Tylenol and rest for a while until feeling better. Nothing can be detected by a regular doctor or hospital if he decides to get checked out. Just another potential to add to the Frequent Flier, Red list!

There has been a great deal of research and analysts at work trying to determine by whom or from where this extremist group is being financed. The issue has been in question for some thirty years or more. It has to be a very secretive and complex network of money laundering or manipulation. Or possibly it could be something that has been a problem right in front of our faces. It could be why this global economic meltdown has happened during the 2010-to-2015-time frame. Could the first multiethnic Arab US president be part of this Muslim Brotherhood movement and secretly financing them? He is the worst president out of all presidents in the history of the United States of America. He has created the highest debt since the Great Depression of the twenties. We're talking like over $20 trillion wasted that was supposed to go to the economy. Aidwantah-Speindyoer-Duolar. (Gov't spenders).

Could this really be a conspiracy of the highest magnitude ever seen? There are still some Communist/Marxist-supported nations that could be sponsoring terrorism to do their dirty work?

Either way, in a couple of short weeks or so, there will be a serious flaw to their positive outcome.

Chapter Six
How Much Is Enough?

After watching civilized countries go bankrupt or close to it, terrorist attacks all around the globe, and the threat of our own nations being compromised, we all knew that we had to do something serious to get these barbaric idiots and the world to listen. When The team's Latin member, Robbie's little niece was murdered when her school bus was blown up, that is what really got us moving. Then there was an embassy massacre cover-up from our own nation's leaderless members. We were receiving donations from unsolicited donors who just felt what was going on was wrong and were just as angry themselves. A sixty-acre ranch in a very rural and rugged area of an Eastern nation was provided by an old farmer. This was also an old WW II underground bunker that the farmer rarely visits. He has offered the entire lot for our use. He will be presented with a nice donation for his retirement.

We had some of our construction crews come in, and with assistance from technology experts and communications techs, they reconstructed underground bunkers that were totally invisible to any modern technological sensors of any kind. Even the cables had a special rubber plastic Teflon coating on them, so there were no stray signals that could compromise the team's position. An old farmhouse and barn were converted into the most high-tech counterintelligence network of capabilities, to prevent any compromise of enemy Counter-Intelligence signal reception of any type imaginable.

The majority of the team's work would be done from the bunker hideout. From flying and watching drones, or UAVs, and what the sensor package on each system provided, it was phenomenal! Another similar offer from another friendly nation in the east came in for site #2!

From underground, water, in the air, or on land, they both had all of the capabilities and more than our nation's own Intel networks used. Thanks to the billions in funding donations and secret contacts that assisted, everything that was needed was obtained. From the military with equipment, modern weaponry, and the newest in high explosives, it was like we were in a storybook. The great minds of specialists who understand this type of warfare could construct prototypes of their own ideas that they knew could have helped them during their own active-duty years. Deployed to many of the same regions or terrain, they could simulate their ideas first, and then have the scientists and technicians construct the real models to practice with and perfect in any areas needed.

Man, are these idiots going to be surprised if and when we can finally finish them!

As Christians and believers in Jesus Christ, the team began to think about the people who were just trying to live their lives under terror regimes. The team wanted to try to provide them with an alternate escape route that would get them closer to the sea or straits. They could send in a mini-UAV/Drone that they could communicate through and tell the friendlies on the ground to inform those families to take only what they could carry for days and any food or water they could bring also. They would all have to pass through multiple sensors that could provide facial recognition and DNA samples. They would look at the sensor drones for a full body and facial recognition, and compile their names into a database of survivors. The mechanized mosquitoes would fly by the person for a photo ID and then get a tiny blood sample for DNA of each person. They would be directed to walk ten feet apart from each other. This way, each sensor device could check and test for any weapons or explosives. An alarm would identify any persons with explosives that had compromised the group. With this plan, the person

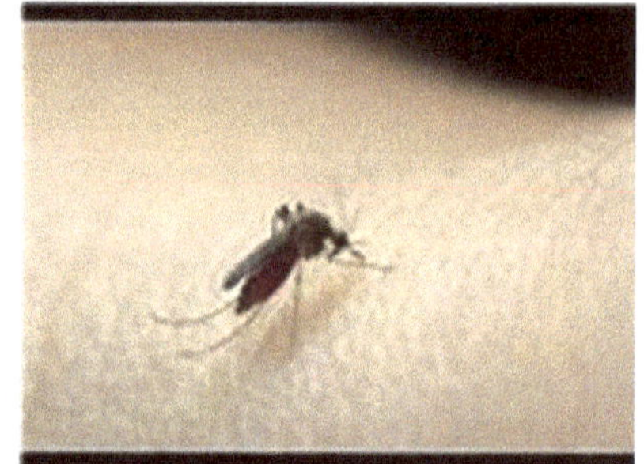

would be tazed to the point that he or she could not move and then be radiated to detonate the explosive. Such people will be left behind to sleep until their graves capsule them permanently.

Security is paramount! In order to crush terrorism, they will need to understand or go to an early meeting with their god.

Who shall be the next target of opportunity? The East, South, West? We can play it all! There are so many new toys to play with. Personally,

I like the guided-slap, explosive-gel type of stick-on explosive, which can be directed straight to a missile launcher detonation system.

Team Jaguar prepares for a mission, while the silent technicians construct more lethal systems that are better and improved from anything ever seen before.

Chapter Seven
Enough Is Enough!

After a global attack from these extremists and all of the death and carnage left behind, someone had to do something. It was beginning to appear obvious that the national leaders either were paid off or playing some part in an unknown conspiracy at this point. But we are definitely going to do something that is going to force the direction of this train to move onto a different railway! The supposed free leader's bowing to Muslim kings? That is proof before your eyes! No one does that unless he is of lesser status than this king and of the same faith. The time is close, and being compromised means that a good warrior would react with speed, surprise, and lethality. In this very nation, many have taken the oath to *"support and defend this nation against all enemies, foreign and domestic."* "Enemies" certainly includes all of the lower-class handout takers and dependents on the government, along with the majority of those of color who felt that they had to eject this Muslim Brotherhood member and sleeper planted in the great land of the free. The erection season is over, and the lazy, lame, dependent citizens have erected this Muslim leader to run out our nation's time clock in another four years. The birthplace of our Lord Jesus Christ for all Christians and believers is surrounded as the extremists are poised to attack our Holy Land. What does this fearless and stoneless leader do? He offers the enemy nations and groups financial assistance to play by his rules to cooperate until all of his chips are in place to do something. And it surely will not be to improve everyone's life in this world. The clock is ticking, and every minute that we lose, they gain. It's time to move!

All that we have heard and read from our news sources is stories of high crimes against our nation and Constitution and cover-ups for embassy attacks and the brutal murders of our ambassadors and security forces that the terrorist group affiliated to Al-Qaeda, the Al Suk Urazz terror group, claimed responsibility for. These attacks are becoming more prevalent around the globe from affiliated terror groups, such as Al-Suk-udria, Aiswar Ama Kweer, and many more. We'll deploy some of our assets to some other operators who have wanted in on this operation badly for a long time. When they attack some of our interests or people, we will retaliate and take out a leader or one of the pissants that are making the calls and giving the orders now.

This could continue forever, but why not take all of the fun that can be had and bring a safer world to all of the other nations that want peace also? We can go about our own business, and the only worry is to keep the government in check.

That is probably asking for too much from other nations that feel that they always need to start some kind of controversy every now and then. Or the loudmouth that has to insist that he be heard about some self-misrepresentation or disrespect.

Another muster is called for an intelligence update and planning review.

Both sites are on their video monitors to listen and see each other. Intel Tommy starts the brief with a classified DOD dispatch marked as "urgent." He begins reading the dispatch that agents in the field and friendly agents have concluded that the Islam extremists are planning to have one of their affiliated terror networks launch a coordinated attack on any remaining NATO embassies that are within the Middle Eastern region. Also, there is a plan to stage a diversionary attack in the Gaza province and then to detonate a dirty bomb in the center of Israel's capital city, Tel-Aviv. France and Italy have had mass transit bombings this week and are threatening retaliation on the groups responsible. Random populated area bombings can make any citizens blood boil in the targeted territory.

Captain Morgan and Pete discuss the possible choices in resetting the timeline.

Captain Morgan says, "Gentlemen, and I use that term lightly, we will need to expedite our movements and actions on the objective area. It would be a great thing if we could do some of these actions on our own. Unfortunately. With this ever-so-evolving and elusive enemy, we must use our technologies to work for us.

"The prisoner cage is exactly that, and we will need to get them out there first and then stage our packages. We will utilize the underwater swimmer devices to slowly maneuver five life rafts into position in the underground canal. Doc is having the blood lab tests completed on each of the prisoners to determine if they are sick or healthy enough to walk the distance to the extraction point. We have requested to Predator to see about coordinating a rescue at sea for some personnel who had been blown off a cargo ship passing in the Gulf area. So far, there has been a delivery sensor vehicle to bring these prisoners a vitamin drink that should provide them with more energy. We will have them out of there, while leaving some stay-behind packages for any guards or retaliating forces. Tomorrow we will have another briefing at 0800. Let's get this job completed so that we can move on to our primary objective. When these prisoners are released and out of harm's way, we will then get started. So, take care for this to be a flawless release, and every station should monitor the evacuation until the rescue ship is seen from our sensors, and then get some sleep! Out!"

Pete replied with, "Roger to all. Everyone, do what we do best, and then get some rest. 2 out!"

Time really didn't seem to exist when being underground by a couple hundred feet or so. Predator felt like he was simply in an office monitoring a computer system.

It was like drawing a line in the sand and saying, "If you cross this, then you are going to get hit hard! Burn our flag? Kill our soldiers and civilians? Disrespect our lives and culture? Not a good thing to do. We will show you soon and get justice for our fallen brothers."

Everyone on this team has lost many friends; some have seen their friends die. They have all been shot more than seven times and have had broken bones and surgeries to repair them. All have something mechanical on them, from prosthetic limbs, implanted pain pumps, screws and ligaments, to tendons reattached.

Pain to these guys is a normal day. It is the honor and integrity that keep them moving, along with strong faith! They all understand that this mission and what they do is not for a paycheck or a media article or story. It is about protecting our beliefs in freedom to pass onto our children and their children. Let's just hope that this natural-looking disaster will make them all stop and think about ever screwing with the alliance again. The hidden secrets and other threats that were said to exist will all be destroyed in this explosion. The terrorist threat will be of a small guerilla ground war if any. Because their main backup threat to global stability by using WMD with chemical or nuclear will be gone.

This entire region will be under surveillance until we see that they have decided to compromise for peace and stability. There are many R&S systems being left behind that can trace and detect future attempts to obtain and cache these deadly weapons. The underworld network will be gone, and now the extremist Muslim groups will have to move in plain sight!

The African Cape will be abolished from the overpressure and shock wave from the detonation in the Indian Ocean and interconnected tunnel network, addressed by their people quickly. Warriors will always exist to protect nations from enemy threats. It is part of human nature, many believe, that there must always be some conflict over leadership, territories, property, and so on. Living, death, and dying are all part of life. It all depends on the culture's way of seeing this in humanity. How can there be a scale or price placed on human life or death? That is possible only in a twisted mind's way of thinking!

So far, Predator has gotten everything prepared for the original plan, the secondary plan, and the contingency plan.

Every good operator has a backup plan for the backup plan.

Every good SOF operator possesses core values, secrecy, the element of surprise, the violence of action, standards of operations (SOPs), and professionalism. Each man had a CBR suit packed in his kit just in case there was an emergency need to use it. But then, everything will run out sooner or later, and God's will, shall prevail overall. Let's hope that this is not needed by these men.

Some say that "life's a bitch and then you die." Maybe these terrorists feel that way, but we sure don't!

Chapter Eight
The Tactical Decision Is Made (H-Hour)

The mapping and calculations for explosive placement were made to allow the correct fire and effect that was desired for this to appear like a natural disaster. Now, having an overlay map showing all of the designated explosive points, tunnel areas, and the extra-special targets of opportunity, everything came together from the countless hours of R&S using the M&M UAV systems, which displayed the entire subterranean network and hidden secrets. With the nuke test facility in range, this in itself would create a total and complete nuclear meltdown of the site and be in the history books as one of the worst natural disaster-caused nuclear reactor meltdowns and explosions in history. Both of the teams' sites are in far European nations, so they would not or at least should not be affected.

Another muster was called this morning. Captain Morgan began by saying, "that everyone should be proud to have carried out this honorable operation, which was very necessary for world peace"!

The Team had connections to U.S. DOD (S&T), Science and Technology Department Testing and Wargaming facilities.

They could wargame the mission to see the effects by providing the technology contacts at the facility with the missions' information and uploading the explosive weight, geological fault line and tunnels.

Being in an enclosed space, the blast and explosives effects could be much higher and cause more destruction. Predator receives feedback from the laboratory that provides computerized imagery from the wargaming tests. The images show the computerized view from the explosive blasts, as well as the earthquake in a real time view! Predator watches the video imagery with shock and pride! Predator says, "Well there you have it"! "Mission complete!"

He calls both Sites onto the big screen to show the Team members just how successful this mission will be and the aftereffects and images of the disaster, as the computer data had provided.

Both sites come online and, Predator greets both Morgan and Pete and tells, "all the members available to muster at the screen, as he describes what they are about to see and just how this was created from the high technology wargaming technology".

Predator tells them, "How the tunnels are blown upwards about 100 feet and then all of the surrounding tunnel's collapse, and the desert geography is annihilated, looking like a crossroads grid from above with fire, smoke and toxic vapors spewing into the air!" "He will play the entire wargaming conclusions and then we will discuss this video and our next planning phase."

He continued, "Predator has been so kind as to coordinate a drop with an Arab-flagged tanker ship. There are some friendly agents onboard who will assist us, and should they fail, Predator will take care of that also. Predator completed his daily coordination plans and then went for his daily one-mile swim. He called a friend, who met him at a café with a small shopping bag. Four boxes of Cohiba #4s! Thank you kindly. Then he picked up a few items from a store and walked into the subway, where he then went into a hidden doorway and utilized his cell phone for rear surveillance. He had small hidden sensors set along his hidden route that could alert him of any intruders—or maybe not.

"The prisoners were released safely and picked up by a German naval vessel in international waters! You will be happy to know that three of those prisoners are friendly fighters from NATO nations' military units. Half of the prisoners were ours! Everything worked like clockwork, and it was an in-and-out operation. 7 prisoners in total. They had been down in that cage for some time it looked like, as thin and dirty as they were.

"Now we can begin with placing the entire powder keg." With that, Captain Morgan turned the briefing over to Joey, George, and B. B. to continue with the details of the setting and priming of the explosive chain that makes up the powder keg. The reactor room would be gone in forty-eight hours, and that should create a Chernobyl effect.

Some nations should not have nuclear weapons or plants!

A high-explosive detonation undersea, 500 pounds or more, on the seabed will be the starting point for detonation and for the earthquake effect, which will include small tsunami warnings in the area. The team plans on using an African/Arab flagged cargo tanker to drop the weapon of determined size and strength and then let the explosive train keep rolling through the INH. A tanker freight ship could push the package off the aft end at night, and it would sink to the bottom of the ocean to the geographic coordinates designated to trigger the seismic activity readings. It will not be from seismic activity; it will just appear that way! Utilizing all of their connections in play, from various supporting nations for peace, the team can use any vessel and fly under any national flag for cover. The first plan is to use a regular freight tanker in international waters to drop the package from the aft end while passing the designated drop point. If they cannot get a Tanker ship, then they will use plan two. This can also be deployed from an airliner that is a freight carrier. This could drop the precious cargo at the coordinates designated by the scientists and geologist.

Then it was time for some relaxation and healing from any injuries and stress. They did have a nice ten-lane Olympic-sized swimming pool and large Jacuzzi to relax in! Captain J. Morgan and Pete quietly passed the message that the primary drop would be from an Arab/African Tanker chartered and piloted by Predators shadow crew to drop the package with no counter surveillance or chance of compromise from a spy in the crew.

Some activity that they had monitored was some researchers with a heavy-equipment unit doing some digging in and around the collapsed zone that followed the geological fault line. They had forgotten or came upon their own nation's cache of explosives or artillery shells that they had commonly used to make the (IEDs), Improvised Explosive Devices that attacked many convoys of our friendly military soldiers, as well as civilians. They sent a very large bulldozer flying about two hundred feet into the air from the blast. Oops!

It was funny to watch from the team's perspective, but probably not for these guys getting a taste of their own medicine. This was a good thing, though, because now no one would try to excavate or get deep soil earth checks. No researchers were going to learn what truly happened here from the fear of their own false intelligence.

The world media was saying, "Earthquake of grand 8.0 magnitude hits Arab world nations, and neighboring nations suffered some damages from tremors and aftershocks. Giant sunken line formed over the Iran-Pakistan underground highway area. National leaders and military are baffled over the crisis. Religious leaders ask the world to pray, thinking that this could be the beginning of the end. World scientists are baffled. They don't know whether to expect more earthquake activity, or perhaps it's all caused by global climate change?"

It is a new beginning, that is certain! Let this day be remembered as a victory December 13, 202?)!

'AMEN.'

Tim, one of the team's intelligence guys, said, "Let me get another Hefeweizen, por favor!" Not being in the United States or territories meant that we could smoke some very good Cuban cigars, which had been sent to us with some of the equipment and rations that had been ordered. It is nice to know some of the people who know you just as well and can insert a few nice boxes of Chiba's into the supplies. Thank you, Predator!

Tomorrow will be some more of the same observation, relaxing, joking, and preparing to get home. The small celebration continued into the early morning hours.

A breaking news report came in that there was a fatal shooting in a shopping mall by a man with two semi-auto pistols. About twenty people were feared dead.

A dirty bomb was blown up in a European transit center. And what made us all jump up was that a school bus of young children was taken hostage by a suicide bomber. The terrorist group claiming this victory or assault against humanity was a splinter group from Ukum ein-Miereer. They have been known to be from the Jordan and Syria regions and are all affiliated with Al-Qaeda and the Muslim Brotherhood!

A media news flash came in on the "immediate" screen, designed for immediate review.

A crazed gunman stormed into an elementary school in New England, like he was going up against an enemy fortress. He had his battle dress on, with Kevlar vest and helmet, a semiautomatic Assault rifle, and two semiauto pistols. He definitely had this preplanned and had enough ammunition on him to wipe out every person in the school. When he heard the sirens from the police responders, he shot himself dead, like the weak person that he really was.

Captain Morgan addressed the team; with Predator listening in. "We will have terrorism in our nation, as well as the mentally ill that snap and do crazy things that are unbelievable. We must never forget what we stand for, just as when we all first decided to join our nation's military and take the oath: 'To support and defend this nation against all enemies, foreign and domestic.' Domestic terrorism is on the rise, and we must always be vigilant of our surroundings and those around us. Let us bow our heads in a moment of silent prayer that someday parents will not have to mourn the loss of their children due to any combat or acts of terror. 'Amen'.

"I believe that we can all agree that we are prepared and ready to move forward with our staging and setup of this planned disaster!"

All the men said, "Hoo-yah," with a loud thunder-like roar! Morgan and Pete told their sites, "To get things ready for full operation". They then had a private meeting with Predator to discuss any last-minute needs or changes. Predator had acquired an Arab-flagged cargo vessel, and he had hired four members to assist with the package and the coordinated drop when it was ordered. Two of the seamen on this vessel would be standing deck security that night, so there should not be any problems. Predator had told them some of what would happen if they did not get this completed, and also, "told them to never speak to anyone of this ever again". The average monthly wages that these men might earn in a business was peanuts compared to what Predator had offered. So, they were more than happy to help. That is exactly how terrorist groups get their help, either by paying or from threats to harm families. Besides, Predator had inserted some of his own sensor drones that could cause a lethal outcome if they failed or were compromised.

Predator, "wished them all well and would be available throughout the mission to assist". Predator out! Morgan, Pete out! "Let the games begin"!

No matter what happened, we could make this work. Predator could set up and coordinate whatever we told him we needed. Participating as a shadow member of the team, Predator had worked with all of the members on the team and had earned his name from running missions in jungle environments. He became invisible in this environment and was feared worldwide by drug cartel members and terrorists who had branched into this area. He was able to walk with a limp from an injury that damaged nerves in his spine. Medical specialists had tried everything that was known to the medical field at that time to try and heal him. He still had his vast knowledge and experience to assist and provide the team with anything needed.

When they all got together to celebrate and have a small reunion, it would be a good thing! Big Al, Steve, and Red all worked with Predator. These guys could be sent over on a minute's notice to provide sniper-suppressive fire or to hold down the enemy patrol to allow the team's equipment to hide again.

We all have a firm understanding that many of our NATO-friendly warfare tactics, techniques, and procedures (TTP) have been compromised and the enemy forces have been through some of our own training at one time or another. We have studied them for decades, just as they have compromised our nation and have some living here as citizens with multiple passports. These are the kind of people that someone would think should be on the red list for suspect frequent fliers. The Internet provides too much information for anyone to see and learn dangerous and deadly techniques, from military training manuals to do-it-yourself home kitchen recipes to make things that the general populace does not have the need to know. Many of these things should be censored from the Internet and public viewing. Even those killing and fight-to-the-death virtual reality Internet games should be restricted from general public viewing. Some younger children who view and play some of these games must walk away with changed feelings or some mental thinking that has been altered from these visions. There is some virtual simulation training that can help a military expert who becomes more proficient from doing this training in place of real live-range training when this cannot be completed due to some reasons such as weather conditions.

In the world news today, there have been some protest marches in a few Arab nations against the Muslim Brotherhood altering the election turnouts to show its candidate as the winner. They are swearing to govern with strict Islam laws and expect people to obey and be compliant. Otherwise, there will be some inner fighting happening if they cannot agree on their rules and laws, wages, and so on. Iran has had protests of nuclear weapons by young men and women in the capital city of Tehran.

There have been some sightings of families moving at night by mule and a cart. At least there are some citizens who have taken in our warnings and are quietly dispersing themselves to the far north or south of the continent. Our night sensors and desert bats are showing families moving and even bringing their herds of sheep! This is a good sign. They know about the nuclear accident and the future planning, which does not mean anything good for their lives there if they were to stay.

George and B. B. asked if they should send in the first large, collapsible spider sensor to check for any booby traps along the route to place the fuse train. Captain Morgan replied, "Roger; deploy sensor." The guys called back, "Roger; sensor deployed." Now they would prepare the man-packs to be moved. The remaining guys, who did not have much to do, sat around the conference room watching the monitors, which showed every sensor site and the INH from their systems. There were a few people dressed in their decon gear and doing something in the reactor room. It looked like they were assembling and setting a remote clock detonation system. These are used for air detonations or to detonate at a known time when it will be in a certain location or facility. This meant that they had something planned— either a test or an actual trial. There was some news about a possible missile test fire from this area soon, supposedly an oversea test flight. We could never have complete trust in what these people say. One thing for certain is that their nuclear test and fission capability is up and running strong! With this earthquake, there should be a time of lost electrical power, like from an EMP weapon. They have so many cables and conduit pipes that run through the tunnels that there is definitely going to be a loss of power and everything that they use.

The Camel spider drone showed that there were no weight-bearing traps or sensor-movement traps that would prevent the mission staging to begin. George and B. B. both reported back to Captain

Morgan. He was in the pool finishing up a PT . "Sir, we have seen no reason for us not to proceed, except for seeing a four-man jeep patrol passing by one of the entrance points close to our insertion. All else is clear!"

George, Joey, Shit-Bag, Al, and the other technicians sent off the first drone, with the charge pallet tethered by a cargo sling. The second drone carried in the first M&M heavy-lift flatbed 4x4. They maneuvered the drones to meet, and the M&M flatbed was set down first. The sling automatically released, and Joey drove it away from the sling and waited for the next drone to set the man-pack onto the flatbed. This was also automatically released from the carrier net, and both drones flew an alternate route to return for the next delivery. Joey was remotely driving the flatbed M&M truck to the first and farthest drop coordinate, closest to the nuke test facility. This site could create the most powerful nuclear detonation of all. We did not know the complete fallout and damage from that. It would still make this all look like a natural disaster caused this catastrophe. Nothing would be heard from these people for some time. And then may it be in peace! As silent as a night air, these vehicles moved with the greatest stealth ability known.

Each of the technicians wanted to drive one of the man-packs to their destination. The man-packs were set in ten- to fifteen-mile intervals. That would mean six more runs. Stealth and precision accuracy was what we needed now! Al and Chuck wanted to play part of this insertion from site #2. They would remotely take charge using their systems to accomplish the same things that site #1 was doing there. Everybody wanted to play!

"As it has always been and should be," Al said to the others. "I did not get all dressed up for nothing. I did not come this far and go through all of this work not to participate. And I didn't come here just to smoke fine cigars and drink with my friends." Everyone laughed.

The last device was finally in place! Captain Morgan called for an all-hands meeting in fifteen minutes. That was 0230 WAT.

Site #2 replied, "Will do; out!" Pete called out on the main space communications. Everyone responded back with, "Roger."

(Draft of overlay map not to scale.)

At 0225, both sites came online to speak to and see each other.

B. B. said to Chuck, "Hey, brother, you're growing a nice salt–and-pepper beard there!"

Chuck replied, "Yeah, and we're not young men anymore, right?"

B. B., having pulled a muscle in his leg from running on the cross-trainer, replied, "You freak in' know that! Predator, are you online?"

Predator's light illuminated, and he replied, "Roger and good morning to all! I have caught a cold from the change in temperature, plus my allergies, and that's been dragging me down some. I'll be fine, and I am looking forward to our holiday party! I want you all to know that we are all set and ready for deploying the big-Un. The ship sets sail in ten hours, so if I can get the absolute definite drop coordinates from you, then I will have it remotely set and brief the assistants to be certain that my instructions are understood. The drop point will be approximately seven miles south from the coast off of the peninsula. This has been the most unstable region of the fault that our models have shown. Let it be perfectly understood that this could actually trigger an actual earthquake! There are many deep valleys and drop-offs that could be close enough to initiate a real quake. I want everyone to be ready to take precautionary measures to be safe if this should spread to other locations."

Joey gave Predator the coordinates, and then it was set. The next time that we would speak, we probably will have heard something from the local news. This could be remotely or manually detonated at any time and date of our choosing.

Having their own private carrier planes at each site, after the mission and the results are viewed, they will write up an After-Action Report (AAR) from each site. Then later, when they physically link up again, they will compare notes and draft the final report for Team Defenders. Morgan asked Pete and every member, "if they would rather pack up our equipment and sensitize the area for return home, or to remain at the sites and watch the full effect on our screens and then redeploy back home"? Everyone elected to remain to have a nice view in a comfortable recliner chair with any kind of their favorite drink and a fine cigar while watching their plan and work function as designed. Being so much as an ocean or sea away, each site was in a safe area and unknown. The chef had scheduled a nice seafood dinner for the team at each site. Lobster tails, stuffed flounder with crabmeat, seared Asparagus, and rice pilaf. Desert was tiramisu or chocolate mousse soufflé. It sounded fantastic. The head chef entered the room and, in a whisper, said, "Compliments from Predator, gentlemen." They all erupted, "All right, Predator, thank you!" There was also a bottle of each man's favorite liquor and mixers, to add a special kick.

Two hours after waking the next day and completing their daily PT, they all entered the conference room. Captain Morgan could see that Pete was online, as was Predator, from their secret sites. "Good morning, all. We all owe Predator for his great coordination and supply efforts to make all of this possible. Is it five o'clock somewhere?"

"Hell, yes," everyone rumbled.

"In approximately two hours and eight minutes, the detonation process should begin. We can see on our timers just how much time is remaining."

('Sometime in the near future.')

At thirty minutes out, they could see Predator light up a Cohiba.

Then at one minute, everyone softly counted down with the timer; or some said a few prayers. Boom could be faintly heard and felt. George said, "6.8 on the Richter scale. Gentlemen, we have an earthquake in the Middle East somewhere!"

One of the monitor screens showed world news. An emergency news flash showed that there had been an underwater earthquake just off of the coast of the Arabian Peninsula, along the Persian Gulf fault line. This also followed across to the west and the Red Sea near Yemen and the horn of Africa. Then from the sensors left behind to self-detonate on their own after the mission and power was turned off from them, the seawater sensor showed some tidal rise. Then the acoustic chain fuse began. Every ten seconds, boom. They were doing tremendous damage to the centuries of hard work, and many hidden secrets were being blown apart and buried!

Four extremists were noticed attempting to flee out of one of the caves. Just as they got twenty feet from the exit, everything collapsed, and they were buried alive. The device that had been set by the nuke plant was probably the largest and most dangerous to the neighboring nations from fallout. It looks like Saddam's hidden WMD's had been located and were triggered near the Jordan and Syrian borders. A shame for them!

Predator said, "Cheers, mates" as he drank some of his Cuba-libre!

"Cheers!" they all responded.

It will be a changed world forever. a cargo tanker, if this plan is not good then they can go to plan#2 to use a cargo aircraft to drop the bundle at the coordinates provided to them.

Chapter Nine
After Action Report. /(AAR).

stated Predator. (Jaguars) final report. Team Jaguars leader, Predator stated,

"This book is dedicated to all of the innocent citizens who have been killed by terrorist attacks and to all of the grieving families that have lost a military member. To the families grieving the loss of a loved one, please say a simple prayer for our military and first responders' deaths from tragic acts of violence or domestic terrorism. We have many new angels and stars in our skies than ever before".

"We live in a very different world from the one we remember from fifty to sixty years ago. We have a Jihad, (Islamic Holy War), declared on us and the NATO Alliance and friendly allied nations. We declared a (G.W.O.T.), Global War on Terror for these horrific, brutal attacks against innocent civilians in America, Israel, etc.!' 'VENGEANCE IS OURS! Always be vigilant and report anything that seems suspicious. Report it to the police. If you and your family are threatened with death or bodily harm or with damage to property, react as you feel is prudent and sufficient to save life and property. Always have an emergency plan and have someone call the police while you focus on the threat that you might be confronting. We have been compromised by these terrorists, as was apparent with the World Trade Center attacks that horrible day of September 11, 2001. As is quoted in the Bible, "We are our brother's keeper." That means that we should care about and look out for one another. We need to remember to teach our children manners and to be polite, to say thank you and you're welcome. We must all live up to the words *respect* and *love*. Parents, hug your children; and children, hug your dads and moms.

(Quote): <u>Winston Churchill;</u> "The farther that we look into the past the better we can see the future." = Learn from "Lessons – Learned."

The End.

R,

Team Jaguar and the author

REF:

1. Internet World Atlas, 12/2012.

2. Wikipedia; Persian Empire research.

3. Koran.

4. Terrorists, Muslim/Islamic Extremism research

5. Publishers images.

6.http://www.mapsofworld.com/images/middle-east-map.jpg.(Free Maps).

7. A vivid imagination and creative thinking of the author.

About the Author

James Matthew Schombs was born in New York, United States of America, in 1963.

He received a BS from Excelsior College and an AA in Liberal Studies from Monterey Peninsula College. He also studying to receive a Certificate of Senior Studies in Terrorism and Counterterrorism Research from Henley-Putnam University.

He worked for the Department Of Defense, (D.O.D.) Contractor as a Counter-terrorism, SOF Analyst with USJFCOM and NATO.

After military retirement, he worked for the Department of Defense as Counter Terrorism, Special Operations Analyst, utilizing a wealth of knowledge of the terrorism base and courses of action from career knowledge and experience along with detailed research and analysis of the (G.W.O.T.); Global War On Terror in a D.O.D. Analyst position and University studies

On September 11, 2001, with hijacked airliners being used as missiles to destroy the World Trade Center and part of the Pentagon, brave passengers scared to death took over Flight 93 and crashed it in an open field in Pennsylvania. The small hijacking team had planned for the Capital Building in D.C.

The Terrorist Anniversary attack was on (09/11/2012), U.S. Embassy Benghazi Libya, attacked by extremists and the entire staff; from the Ambassador and 3 bodyguards are they accountable to the President and Washington, D.C. They have done nothing!

This book is in memoriam to all of the innocent passengers, police, firefighters, and emergency rescue people who lost their lives on September 11, 2001. Our military has fought relentlessly against these terrorists, and all military service members, veterans and patriotic

American citizens are extremely grateful for their sacrifices and selfless acts of heroism in combat. Bless these warriors and their families!

Is Team Jaguar fact or fiction? You decide.

Predator thought that the people should know the truth about what has happened and is now happening. This story could be fact or fiction. I have placed it in the fiction category.

Let your imagination take you there! Go, Team Jaguar!

God bless America!

An extra map of the Middle East that I had paid for online.